CW01395347

Th

The Acts

Richard Barrett
Steve Hanson

Dostoyevsky Wannabe Experimental
An Imprint of Dostoyevsky Wannabe

First Published in 2018
by Dostoyevsky Wannabe Experimental
All rights reserved
© Richard Barrett and Steven Hanson

Dostoyevsky Wannabe Experimental is an imprint of
Dostoyevsky Wannabe publishing.

Cover Design by Victoria Brown & Richard Brammer.
dostoyevskywannabe.com

ISBN-13: 978-1722830762
ISBN-10: 172283076X

'An act is not to be compared with an animal movement, but a human thing and only a human thing. Humans can be held responsible for them. This happens all the time in courts of law. There is, therefore, an ethic of acts. However since Freud, and then Lacan, we must add to the conscious decision to act the unconscious structure of these human acts. Freud found "parapraxes" or "bungled actions" to be proof of a live, operating unconscious human dimension. The bungling is in fact only in error for the conscious side of the split subject. The fuckup is the triumph of the unconscious. Do we take responsibility, then, for our unconscious? For those other ragged drives that have us riven up inside? Lacan suggests that because the unconscious desires are only ever expressed in warped form in the "civilised" human suicide is the only completely successful act.'

– Hedwig Mendelssohn reads to the other postgraduate students from the Dictionary of Lacanian Psychoanalysis

Index

Act 1: Hatred and War (postponed)

My old English literature teacher used to say 'always begin with a tragedy'. The roots in Homer, The Odyssey and Iliad. But I never believed her. So I'm not able to keep it up. Or at least keep a straight face. In any case, romance and tragedy are now inseparable:

Act 2: Love and Happiness

Claudia: *Pizza, Swimming, Harley Davidson +12*

Fatima: *Relaxing, Internet +2*

Gail: *The Circuit, Emmerdale, Sunday Roast +29*

Anna: *Sunglasses, Hanging out, Weekend trips +497*

Natalie: *Shrek, Jokes, Walking +38*

Sammy-Joe: *Sun, Romance, Johnny Depp +20*

Gaynor: *Relaxing, Football, The Lion King +25*

Vicki: *Hollyoaks, Disney +15*

Michelle: *Wine, Cinema, Greek Islands +14*

Claudia: *Vodka, Berlin, George Clooney +109*

Act 3:

We are in Manchester. Like many others, our homes have been carved from mammoth blocks of clean white Citalopram and Sertraline. We live inside and on our worst days nibble away at the skirting boards and door frames. The black slab in the corner burbles and foams. White foam. Black foam.

As the street drinkers in the Godot of our fantasies I only prefer Sertraline, my Spesh to your Tenants Super.

Our tenancies: White corridors cut from the chalky substance; like the black slab, it is ultimately cheap, ultimately expensive and no contradiction here.

'The Haçienda must be built' was coined by Ivan Chtcheglov the poor, half-mad Situationist, who was arrested en route to the Eiffel Tower with armloads of dynamite, intent on blowing it up because its lights kept him awake at night.

It was once tempting to declare that Engels urgently

needs to return to Manchester to observe the homeless situation, but after the nauseating siting of the Engels statue outside HOME to jubilant crude Marxist cheering maybe Chtcheglov needs to come to Manchester for the first time to detonate its myths. Blast them into atoms so tiny that the original stories can no longer be read.

In 2018, the thing wanted is proving utterly impossible to just go out and get, dependent – entirely – on the whim or else carefully considered decision of the other person, perhaps the Haçienda must be finally demolished.

The building has gone but its myth casts a shadow across the city that stops people from seeing 'Person A' and 'Person B': with 'Person A' being a woman and 'Person B' a man, or vice versa, and vice versa.

It's about power always and forever. So whether it's a bloke who only comes round on a Sunday; and not every Sunday at that, asking 'shall we go for a drive?', meaning, 'are thaa up for a shag in the backseat in half an hour?'; or whether it's a woman unable to say the word love to the one who's been saying it to her for months but what does she care as she's leaving town the beginning of next year anyway and won't be providing her forwarding address, whether it's a woman or a man is irrelevant, matters not a bit, has nothing to do with anything in this North of England Orlando versioning, referring to not the book but, rather, the Tilda Swinton starring, Sally Potter movie adaptation from whatever year it was from.

These stories, now flattened a millimetre thin by their endless circulation, conceal richer ones. But the digression is important as analysts know. We are trying to get at something here.

Bob Dickinson told us that the late, brilliant Alan Wise told him that the force of the blast of the 1996 IRA bomb created a space of physics inside the legendary red post box that was, momentarily, a gateway to another dimension. This 'fact' was apparently 'read somewhere' – in an article by an Indian physicist which was eventually mislaid. Manchester Area Psychogeography levitated the Corn Exchange only months before the bomb. Just over the way from this post-box-stargate is the Waterstones where Jeff Noon worked: Totally independent of Alan Wise, *The Raw Shark Texts* by Steven Hall posits a portal to another universe in Deansgate Waterstones. Peter Barlow's Cigarette, a literary event sometimes hosted there, takes place within this zone of Pure Weird. You can go and have a coffee there. The Sober and The Space Cadets are one here, yet Manchester can't seem to produce a single decent radical independent bookshop at its centre.

We live in *Satan's Brew* by Fassbinder, in *La Vie de Boheme* and *Calamari Union* by Kaurismaki. Which one of us is the fly-collecting brother changes from hour to hour, but we are both always already the reincarnation of Stefan George.

Demolition Polka, written when George was three years old, was a popular Strauss waltz, as cities exploded in the nineteenth century. We see again how the risk and hedging of capital have turned our public spaces into Demolition Poker, with Pomona seceded to banality and Rogue Studios sold off to developers. The city is being ripped up and re-laid under our feet again, and so perhaps we need to re-enter this game with rigged cards, or new strategies.

What are the literary equivalents of Set-Mining, The Reverse Tell, The Soul Read, The Stop and Go or The Triple-Barrel Bluff? Manchester needs new Magic. But it needs new myths that the capitalists cannot swallow.

In fact, it needs stories that will make them choke and turn bluer than they already are.

Here are some.

So comfort scoff an entire tub of Stella Artois

flavoured ice-cream and listen.

Or else, if sick of listening, go do the thing that makes you you. Go write a poem or whatever; think about writing a poem before remembering you don't do much of that these days and so, instead, put a DVD on.

White Keys

'Ulrich could never stand this piano, always open and savagely baring its teeth, this fat-lipped, short-legged idol, a cross between a dachshund and a bulldog, that had taken over his friends' lives even as far as the pictures on their walls and the spindly design of their arty reproduction furniture...'

- Musil, The Man Without Qualities

The Spinster

Richard, occasionally we will need to consult The Spinster. E.P. Niblock, or 'The Spinster Fabulista'. An early poet of Manchester Concrete, her interests and obsessions predate 'brutalists' such as Owen Hatherley, tallying with her friend LoneLady, with whom she lived in Brunswick Tower, in Ardwick, Manchester. What we need from The Spinster is her background in archeology. She describes Manchester as a 'young city', as a cocky young upstart. This may seem surprising to those who view the place as the ancient origin of the modern. Her diaries and letters appear to mix up time, they are simultaneously modern, Victorian, of the contemporary and past, in one place: Manchester. The Spinster has transformed herself into a mixture of Margaret Rutherford, the Victorian Bluestocking and the multiverse heroines of science fiction, particularly Catherine Cornelius and Una Persson, a female flaneuse predating the current vogue for such things by at least twenty years (for instance Elkin, 2016).

As has been pointed out elsewhere, via Michael Keith's work on the subject, anger is not allowed in academia, but nor is humour, as Cormack, Cosgrave and Feltmate pointed out in 2017. The Spinster's writing addresses the city through irritation, but also with humour. Thus, she has been scandalously denied her rightful place in the university. Where The Spinster diverges from the current Modernist script is that she is critical.

I can see from her Letters that our scene is well-described:

'The snow continued. The moon, a cutlass slash in an ink-black sky, glittered over an icebitten Brunswick more Brothers Grimm storyboard than inner city estate; the Mancunian Way a sinuous white river, cars drifting silently by; the graveyard usually windswept and forlorn now a Byronesque ruin; common or garden urban decay transformed into fields of arctic wilderness, desultory barbed wire fences an armoury of stalactite daggers.'

But she will only now speak to us in Angel language, from exile, like Goytisolo, looking back from Tangier to Franco's Spain. She gazes at our mainland reality with ambivalence and a critical eye… she will temper what we will later describe as our 'male trodding…'

Act 4:

Or THE BACHELOR AKA Unfilmed Michael Haneke script #1.

Starring Ben Affleck as an unlucky in love singleton who spends every Saturday night alone, crying into his glass of Polish lager at his loneliness, rehearsing, in his mind, the conversation he'll have later with the girl who will answer his call to the suicide hotline, and who, after that, will go out and solve a murder. Highly relatable.

Will Ben have found someone by the final act?

(A girl on a chair in a room. The room isn't important; neither is the chair, though more details about both may well be provided later; the girl is important: What the girl is thinking, what her past is which has fed into what she's thinking right now, both those things are important. She sits not looking at the wall opposite her, her head is merely facing in that direction, facing in your direction: you... the 'you' of all the millions of unwritten poems plus all those irregularly and obscurely published; that 'you'. Am I that you, the girl wonders?)

Upton Speaks

'My dear cyborgs, this talk is taken from a larger piece of writing in which I address my own collaborations; and issues relating to the inter-relationship of many areas of artistic activity, particularly Poetry, Music and Painting; as well as the music and commentary of Cornelius Cardew...'

- interlude (meanwhile) –

52m ago Egypt FM to head to Ethiopia after Nile dam talks stall

1h ago Fire in Philippine shopping mall kills 37

1h ago Vice Media co-founders apologise for 'boy's club' environment at firm

2h ago Bundesbank says no euro zone cryptocurrency in sight

2h ago Rescuers search for Philippine storm victims as toll rises to 200

3h ago North Korea says new U.N. sanctions an act of war

4h ago China closes more than 13,000 websites in past three years

7h ago Venezuela freeing some jailed activists, may expel diplomats

7h ago Federal judge partially lifts Trump's latest refugee restrictions

10h ago Mexico murders hit record high, dealing blow to president

11h ago Myanmar, accused of crackdown, invited to U.S. - Thai military exercise

11h ago Russian communists drop veteran, select surprise candidate

11h ago Russia's ruling party seeks Putin's 'ultimate victory' at 2018 election

42 i:

The production of what became known as 'the forty-twos' began after he attended the Ernst Bloch retrospective conference under the pseudonym 'Hedwig Mendelssohn', a doctoral candidate at Baden-Wurtemburg on Goethe and Melancholia.

This conference took place at the University of Durham in early 2015. He went up there with Mark Rainey, on the train, getting up at 6am, after spending the night in Castlefield, in the bed of a Russian music promoter he had been seeing.

A dead Christmas tree rolled under the railway bridge like tumbleweed, as more snow fell.

Mendelssohn had been granted the go-ahead for his task of re-writing the King James of 1611 in materialist form, for which he had just signed a contract with Repeater, and at that point this was due in six months. Mendelssohn was 'off on the sick', his department had paid the conference fee, but he needed detailed notes for his new work, and so I had to travel up there on his behalf, meeting figures such as Michael Koch, Peter Osborne, Michael Raubach and Canon Andrew Shanks.

Although Mendelssohn was well on with his new biblical work, it had completely eclipsed his previous writing project, a fictional retelling of the latter stages of 2014, entitled '42', no age to be during this troubled period, yet the age he was.

- interlude (Hatred and War, still postponed) -

'The latest U.N. sanctions against North Korea are an act of war and tantamount to a complete economic blockade against it, North Korea's foreign ministry said on Sunday, threatening to punish those who supported the measure. The U.N. Security Council unanimously imposed new sanctions on North Korea on Friday for its recent intercontinental ballistic missile test, seeking to limit its access to refined petroleum products and crude oil and its earnings from workers abroad. The U.N. resolution seeks to ban nearly 90 percent of refined petroleum exports to North Korea by capping them at 500,000 barrels a year and, in a last-minute change, demands the repatriation of North Koreans working abroad within 24 months, instead of 12 months as first proposed. North Korean leader Kim Jong Un on Nov. 29 declared the nuclear force complete after the test of North Korea's largest-ever ICBM test, which the country said puts all of the

United States within range. Kim told a meeting of members of the ruling Workers' Party on Friday that the country "successfully realized the historic cause of completing the state nuclear force" despite "short supply in everything and manifold difficulties and ordeals owing to the despicable anti-DPRK moves of the enemies". North Korea's official name is the Democratic People's Republic of Korea (DPRK).'

Act 5:

The I heart Manchester logo, seen on out of service buses, always carries a residue - no matter how much the heart swells it cannot inflate far enough to expel all of it so that the last trace of xenophobia is pushed out like bad air, it is always present...

Act 6:

Non-E gr. Categories. Kwaki. 'Eskimo'. Sioux... (Boaz). Thig Thag Thob Thuzzle. Whorf, overt gr.

categories and covert gr. Categories. Cryptotypes vs. phenotypes.

The Fatberg. Wet wipes, toilet tissue, condoms, nappies, toothpicks, tampons. Zizek describes ideology as shit, but the fatberg is a sign of the all-pervasive presence of ideology. Of toilet training beyond toilet training. Human blubber peppered with all the technologies of 'bio': Wet wipes, toilet tissue, condoms, nappies, tampons and toothpicks. Wipe off, capture, prise out and separate the good from bad.

These are actions that mirror the linguistic attempts to do the same thing that are inscribed in the very form of language, a binary system of difference that is cultural, not natural. All the myriad daily actions of 'civilization'. The greyer areas can be seen in the kitchen, for instance the decision to use one sponge for the washing up and one for the surfaces. A distinction is being made, that the sink and surfaces are not equally contaminated, that one is dirtier than the other; ideology.

And now, in London, not in Manchester, there is a Fatberg exhibition. Not only the drains but the history of drains are ideological. At MOSI in Manchester the Roman Sewer exhibit, collaged into everything else, in a remote and under-attended part of the complex, provides a worthwhile place for the readers of this text to reflect on what has been said so far.

Act 7: so speaks 'the girl' aka Michelle

In this chair, in this room, alone or with somebody else... I know that all writing is presentation; an attempt to show the self in the light most favourable. I know this is as true of every poem I have written as it is of every Tweet I have drafted and posted or maybe deleted. Writing is a new item of clothing. Every 'you' that I write is written only after having carefully consider how that 'you' will reflect upon me. The 'you's' of my writing are vacancies then, really;

vacancies that I fill with the immeasurably important 'me', who is 'I', the author of these words, the co-author of these words, co-authored with the thoughts and feelings of my body and brain which grow and develop in accordance with each of my interactions in the world, making it reasonable – therefore – to claim as the co-authors of this work everyone I/we have ever met, or in some other way encountered.

The ultimate goal of all this effort towards presenting oneself well being to FEEL OKAY.

I want to FEEL OKAY.

I want to turn this computer off and go into the other room where my partner is to spend time with them. I want to go to the gym. I want to go to the kitchen and start eating and realise I have no good reason to stop eating. I want to win fame and accolades for my writing. I want to leave an ever-lasting mark upon the culture. I want to watch something daft on telly which I don't have to think about. I want to double the dose of my anti-depressant. I want to half the dose of my ant-depressant. I want to phone my friend.

I don't want to feel like shit.

Trying to figure out how to make that happen.

Act 8: Fragument

On the path behind the shitty old flats from the second floor of my office building by the window. Sat shifting figures from one column to another trying to reach some kind of conclusion I feel satisfied with. The road is visible through the trees and I am walking on it and anticipating it; knowing that, soon, ahead, there will be the high-sided bridge over the railway line; knowing that figures such as that are having your legs broken figures that I am now crossing over, noting the graffiti now, on my way to Pete's, the light of the late afternoon bouncing off the water and reflecting onto the office ceiling. The road is visible through the trees and on Codexmaps in some greatly reduced electronic form on Codexmaps.

I mean, not in the sense of an identification number of some kind; I mean, rather, a mathematical object made from many other mathematical objects: an accumulation or an aggregation of mathematical objects dissolving into the light on the office ceiling caused by the sun hitting the water outside. A number dissolving into light it seems this late in the day; situated here in this field of mathematical possibilities and impossibilities on this posture-paedic chair I inherited, designed for expectant mothers.

Divided and divided and divided until nothing is left; until night falls and the assassins with calculators have dispersed, laughing; happy at their sums all having worked out right. I am less than and will only become even more reduced. The night in Piccadilly when the life-stories of everyone passing by were suddenly and unexpectedly revealed to me; me having to make no effort whatsoever to know the whole lives of all those people. How, around that time, all that strange shit kept happening: the whispered messages from the cityscape of Manchester at dusk; the repeated illuminations in the terraced house's back room... The line from then to now which, really, isn't any kind of line at all. The multiplicity of such invented and imaginary lines in the biography of a person.

That, this late in the day... drifting into the night sky thusly heard by occupants of the nearby flats as the mating cry of some strange, unknown breed of animal, their mournful chants. The ritual of the midnight river-bank; the necessity of that ritual. The bowed heads over the mass graves. Night and the shadows and watching taking place, occurring, in the absence of, even, any discernible subject. The leaves of the trees and the ground level foliage rustling. The wild girl of Manchester, all ten of them, see and the wild girls know...

My dissolve into mathematical un-hood from the

beginnings of my entirely plagiarised person, the constituent elements spottable by anyone with keen enough eyes. Trying, my very hardest, to make these figures balance – this is my existence during daylight hours. Knowledge of the consequences for the universe of the failure to achieve that balance. Columns and rows and columns and rows. The big data of occult bookkeeping. What time is it? Is it the sun or the moon above me on the office ceiling or perhaps my own reflection that I am falling in love with? Yet no-one seems to be calculating the hourage of those who are calculating the hourage. The failure to fulfill an obligation, to appear, pay, or act in some way. Lack, absence, a pre-selected option fallen back upon. Our downsize ratio, what we've ended up with. A million unpaid for phone calls. Those tautologies were always irrelevant to nature, and now they have even less meaning, but the hourage calculators haven't quite caught up, engaged as they are, in the calculation of hourage. A million noughts is still zero. I am a bank vault of quixotic inconstancy, obstinate patterns and lusts. My report and accounts finds me rich in all of the intangibles, dripping with them. Haven't I said all of this before?

My id is banging at the fucking lid today.

That building didn't exist yesterday. A pyramid crashed there early this morning and to keep that secret they quickly constructed that building around the pyramid's still visible above ground pointy tip.

Two consecutive lines with the same words beginning them.

I feel as a deserted concrete shopping plaza from the early 80s.

I feel as a deserted concrete shopping plaza from the early 80s.

Doctor, I…

Act 9: restored scene

The corridor which brings you from outside in; which brings you across the landing to your apartment; ill lit in places; not somewhere you'd want to linger; a kind of nothing place, neither here nor there really… This is a corridor we've entered in the full knowledge that it's not going to take us home; that we're going to be perfectly safe in it and that in a very short space of time we'll emerge into the next part of this nice idea; a small taste of what life is like in a nice, spacious, modern building having exchanged our awareness of just exactly where we are and where we'll soon be remaining as we walk, hung on the wall to our left, seemingly, 70s or 80s vintage wallpaper. With the turn of the corridor in sight, and with it, we expect, the opening out into the next room, we stop and look at the wall display: the images we are seeing are the landscape the person telling their story existed in; perhaps it's the landscape which would be visible from this corridor if it was really just around the corner.

- After Labyrinth (My Mother's Album),

Ilya & Emilia Kabakov

Dub 1:

It was forever ago. For occupants entering, I will the contravention 'pon thaa, the ever old contravention. The item that twitched for the fan systematically. She's of the day and the Manchester pothead, the Citalopram-go owners, watching for the inspired buy. The Me that talks of The Problem, The Losses, moves gold on, rather than checks the old songs: Here they even empty the inside wins; they are uncertain of most of the field.

42 ii:

To understand all of this more fully, we need to track back a couple of years: When Mendelssohn reached 40 years old, he took stock, sketching out a project called 'Life begins at forty', or, 'beginning in the middle, a twenty year project'. Mendelssohn was still finishing his PhD at that point, and though this would take another six months to write up and submit, he decided that it was time to start thinking about another long-term project, aside, of course, from irritating pointless day jobs. He had been talking to Simon Ford, who now explains wearily, for the record, that Mendelssohn frequently and angrily stated his intent to 'declare what I am doing for at least the next two decades'.

Just before his fortieth, Mendelssohn made a playlist of forty songs, one for each year of his existence, each song made within the island he lived upon. Suddenly, out of that bit of indulgence, play, essentially, Mendelssohn quickly generated a timetable for a representational project which would involve going over his previous forty years during the next twenty, as well - as a matter of course, literally - as he went over the next twenty at the same time. This would, if pulled off, cover all of his life up to sixty years old, at which point, he could take stock and re-strategise.

The timetable he generated, in one sitting, indicated what year he would be in and what years he would have to cover, representationally, during those years. The timetable he created runs as follows:

[40] 2012 - 2010/11 [38/39]

[41] 2013 - 2008/09 [36/37]

[42] 2014 - 2006/07 [34/35]

[43] 2015 - 2004/05 [32/33]

[44] 2016 - 2002/03 [30/31]

[45] 2017 - 2000/01 [28/29]

[46] 2018 - 1998/9 [26/27]

[47] 2019 - 1996/7 [24/25]

[48] 2020 - 1994/5 [22/23]

[49] 2021 - 1992/3 [20/21]

[50] 2022 - 1990/1 [18/19]

[51] 2023 - 1988/9 [16/17]

[52] 2024 - 1986/7 [14/15]

[53] 2025 - 1984/5 [12/13]

[54] 2026 - 1982/3 [10/11]

[55] 2027 - 1980/1 [8/9]

[56] 2028 - 1978/9 [6/7]

[57] 2029 - 1976/7 [4/5]

[58] 2030 - 1974/5 [2/3]

[59] 2031 - 1972/3 [0/1]

So, for instance, when we look down the table, to 2021, when Mendelssohn will be forty-nine years of age, he will have to look back to 1992 and 1993, in 2021. He will be accounting for the 1992-3 period, which at the moment are fairly fresh, but by 2021 will be quite distant, as history will have moved further. This is one way, it was hoped, in which the timetable of practical work as laid out would militate against narcissistic, excessively close representation, at the same time as it could provide a concrete framework for operation.

Of course, all writers are autobiographical workers to some extent. The writer is in the text to a greater or lesser degree, even after the supposed 'death of the author', and so Mendelssohn decided that he needed to not just simply admit that, but actually make it central to his project. This said, there is a clear need to avoid narcissism, solipsism and indulgence. So his new long-term project should be autobiographical, but outward-looking. Sniffing back over the trail of his own life, Mendelssohn discovered that there were already scraps of evidence, pieces of writing, paintings and photographs, from, say, 1990, and even if the painting was now lost, there were photographs of them, as there were photographs of lost girlfriends. There will be a way in which they could be brought back, via the present, into the future, transformed.

Nothing is lost, that they are is the only fiction.

There are two systems of time working at once here, what Iain Sinclair explained to Mendelssohn in 1998, when he interviewed him: Quick, present time - the time of making representations in the immediate moment, which congeal that same year, dry like oil paint - but also two other years which get increasingly distant as the project goes on. Put simply, Mendelssohn was going to 'do something' with the year he was in, and two earlier years, each year, for twenty years.

So, 2010-12 was meant to be the smashed dead centre. The recent experiences of mid-life were supposed to be collated representationally, as the crash of 2008 reached the eye of its storm. As the representations he made moved out, they were to then inevitably diverge, formally, as if moving out from this calm centre, into a maelstrom. It is a planetary practice. Mendelssohn would be navigating the blasted cosmos of his own existence, finding orbital debris, evidence of this named figure, the only clues he has to go on. Its exponential geographical-representational aspects were mirrored in Spinoza's ethics and its pseudo-geometric form, as was the essay in the first edition of his biblical work.

If he got to the end of the project, those pieces could then be laid out chronologically - if required - and edited into a single whole of some sort. He would be on the cusp of his sixties when he reached the years of his birth, so best not leave it too late, he figured. He might not get it all done, but if that were the case his own death would be part of the work.

If he got to sixty, Mendelssohn figured, he would then begin making representations on the years before his own lifespan and after it, out into both the future and the past, into zones where and when he never existed and never will: Then the plot would really thicken.

One needs, like a good orchestral conductor, to begin

on this kind of work after 60 in any case. There is no point tackling such things before that age, even if one reaches it in a fit state to do so.

This is when one should begin painting (oh *fuck off*). But after finally finding and describing his 'system', the thing he had been searching for all his life, Mendelssohn let two years elapse without working on the project. He became Jonah. He heard his calling and he wandered abroad, but in the wrong direction (see above re Russian music promoter, and the other ones). He damned his fellow passengers and his subsequent swallowing was utterly real. This work is the whale's belly. But this work is also the way out of the whale. Mendelssohn, in evenings off from his biblical re-write, would now have to work on the years he missed. Mendelssohn had also published his first book, New Communities of The Sad Spirit, which was researched during the 2006-12 period: Those years were close by and should incur no major representational distortions.

The agreement was this: As Mendelssohn does these works of penance, Barrett would work on 'forty-two', with access to the Lavery and Hassall, who knew Mendelssohn during this period. Barrett was to work on his dead centre for him, with these two defrocked priests, like father, son and holy ghost, as if they were a team of masseurs, intervening just as his real muscles were about to pull.

So here begins the twenty year project of 'representations', starting from the middle, Deleuze says something along those lines. Iain Sinclair described getting a long way into a journey to see time open like swan's wing, instead of all this 'male plodding'. Things get thick, the past is being retrodden, as new experiences pass, and also thickened by the accumulation of experience, but via this, paradoxically, it also opens out for you, its shape, its beauty and power, become clear.

Upton Speaks

'At a party, I found myself in "the music room" in front of an electronic keyboard. I began playing. I drew an audience. My hostess finding herself alone elsewhere in the house and also hearing the music, came in, saw me, and expressed surprise with "Lawrence? What are you doing? You can't play keyboards." I replied: "Clearly, I can." to which she responded "But you're not a musician." 7 or 8 years before, when I had taken up postgrad study of Computer Science, she exclaimed "But you can't. You're a poet."'

Act 10:

Contentment, repose of the heart, a harmonious village in which all the inhabitants are me. Good loyalty and faithfulness… inverted… roguery, deception, project voided, bad faith. Lost: The World Assured, success, voyage, change of place. Good advice probably rejected through to slander and babbling, an old and vicious man, ugliness, perversity, corruption, peril, impudence, extravagance, dispute with an imbecile. This is good but severe advice that should be followed to prosperity, beauty, increase. Tim Berners-Lee, the surety of possession and gifts. The final stage of action, reflection, thoughts and deeds. It heralds the end of a cycle, the natural winding down or closing stages of a period of life. Fours are peaceful and grounded, ruled by the Emperor.

Act 11: Date Night, alone

The path to Haneke. However many films he's made that I've let pass, uninterested. I want an activity that has no meaning beyond itself. An activity that I can engage in with no thought as to how the activity is going to/might at some future point go on to feed into my art. I am so sick of poetry knowing, as I do, that the only question a person has to resolve in their time on earth is the question of how to best spend their time; how to do least harm to others whilst, simultaneously, maximizing their own enjoyment levels... until, eventually, the Haneke-shaped gap in my film viewing history began to seem problematic, somewhat. You don't help yourself. I don't help myself. She doesn't help herself. Why watch such miserable films when you're so goddamned miserable yourself all the time. You don't help yourself. She doesn't help herself (see above).

Beginning with the 'Glaciation' trilogy. Each film opening with the remembered scene from the poetry workshop held in the basement bar a long, long time ago; always the same but different; the blank look of incomprehension at the presentation of the printed-out A4 sheet. "I don't get it". They don't get it... a news broadcast, either from the radio or the black slab: a contextualizing of all that follows the moment of the lone bright spark finally chirping up with 'I think it's that the "I" isn't fixed; it's fluid, unstable, an "I" that signifies numerous subjectivities, sometimes contradictory...' plus an ambiguous cause and effect argument with those designations refusing, determinedly, to remain fixed.

Consequently, the low sigh of understanding from the man's neighbor travels around the circle of those assembled; now, perhaps, they get it. The poem is picked-up by each again; looked at again. 'Yes, that's right; that's the key', violence that comes after... the man said: '...Tilda Swinton even, against persons unknown, known and the self' and eventually, shockingly, disturbingly, violence against possessions. The horror of watching a family systematically destroy every item that they own; a horror unsurpassed by the knowledge that that destruction will be followed, one by one, by the eventual deaths of each member of the family. The horror of understanding the greater shock you feel is caused by seeing brand name goods being smashed up.

Film Comment calling Haneke a pious admonisher.

I am not the sum total of the things I have bought and so now own; on the other hand, though, what I actually am is often unclear.

'I should go and write a poem about all of this' I think, they thinks, she thinks (some habits DIE HARD). The moment she felt the impulse to write a poem, though, was the very same moment she felt that impulse die. Instead she put a film on, Michael Haneke's fourth.

Act 12:

Plague of RIPs all over The Circuit when a pop-star or black slab celebrity dies. A phenomenon I've never understood and which always leaves me feeling uneasy.

They're looking for meaning, because it's been pulled out from under them as one might pull up a sapling and chuck it on the floor by its hole. It has as much chance of re-rooting on its own as they do finding meaning in the Death of Bowie, Prince, the Gods of God-oh.

The Christmas tree follows Mendelssohn all the way under the arch. He has visions of it rolling all the way to Victoria Station with him.

Upton Speaks

'*I have moved towards hybridity in my collaborations with John Levack Drever. Both artists are working in an intermediate area which shares aspects of Poetry and Music and Visual Art. It is not not Poetry. I am interested in giving it a new name. Both of us are actively making the work. It is not Poetry & Music, which I call cooperation; but a totality of making for which I reserve the word collaboration.*'

42 iii:

Back at the conference in Durham, the discussion settled on Gillian Rose's concept of the 'broken middle', and it was clear that Mendelssohn was in his own broken middle, in 2014, and like John, the figure he was transmuting like shit into gold, he was broken, his faith had gone, but via his alchemical work he was regaining ground, slowly. He was still convinced that any biography must be written in and of the broken middle, and not from the beginning to the end, or at the end, as some ponderous, pompous, self-satisfied retrospective from an armchair by a blazing fire. This final scenario was not in any way guaranteed. But what needed to happen, urgently, desperately, life-savingly, was the re-instatement of the twenty-year plus project.

So, while speaking to Hassall, who had been Mendelssohn's informal Attorney for some time, a suggestion arose that I could feed, via him, The Facts, for libel-checks if nothing else, to Professor Carl Lavery. Lavery is an expert on literature, theatre and the absurd. My aim was for it to be written up as fiction and be published in some collaborative manner. Barrett would then tear these up blindfold and glue them into the work at hand.

I was beginning to suspect, correctly, that Mendelssohn was far too close to the material of his own existence in 2014, particularly the traumatic elements, to really allow the absurdity and humour to emerge. What he sent to me suggested this strongly. Mendelssohn, in any case was not available, so the proposal was to email the bare, sordid details over, drip by drip, a reversal of what is assumed to be the usual twenty first c. process, pure Fact masquerading as a zone of sheer fabulation.

Do not call this 'Metamodernism' the 'New Sincerity' or 'truthiness' because of that reversal. Do so at your peril. Do so, and I will break into your house as you sleep and shit in your expensive brogues.

The facts-as-fabulation are given so that others might then set about making it into a narrative with all the correct romantic flourishes. It should be more romantic, not less. I could then insert Mendelssohn's already completed, crucial occult material, find a publisher, and prepare the printer's manuscript, perhaps adding some jokes about farting.

Squatting down, jeans around my thighs, squeezing the sloppy coil into the foot-sized leather hole.

It should probably be noted that Mendelssohn is a hybrid of an eternal, badly-behaved six year old, a militant, rough working class shop floor labourer, a highly developed, nuanced academic, and the benign creator-deity of the cosmos, although he still gets tax warnings and other bureaucratic trivia. I'm not sure why that is. His work for The Party also continues and is mentioned in the text occasionally.

As this process went on, it became clear that a radically edited, abridged version of this discourse was all that was required: The process of negotiating, editing and writing were the final work. Because Mendelssohn's status as a writer who deals with various bureaucratic agencies and troublesome editorial figures - academic, secular or other - is part of his very fabric, and so it should be part of his 'biography', 'experimental autoethnography', call it what you will. The trinity of Attorney, Editor and Writer was in any case real, and how the text you hold was generated.

I have had enough of this. I initially considered referring to you collectively as 'The Editors'. But Lavery, you are Edit-or, The Llavourer. Hassall you are Attorney: I do not know if it is an omen for good or ill that this fiction already needs the defibrillator of other fictions. Please advise. I shall henceforth, magical name or no, be called I, or 'I am', as in The Great I Am and none greater, or I can even be referred to by this... this 'word'... this 'Mendelssohn'. Spit it out, as I do, with total contempt.

The key for this discourse is as follows: I am 'I'; Hassall, 'Attorney'; Lavery, 'Editor'; Barrett, here, is 'Richard' or in recourse to traditional pictorialism, 'Barrett'. 'Hanson', sidelined, will be referred to as such and in the latter stages only, utterly peripheral as he is to this work.

This said, the vernacular, colloquial and vulgar names these fantastical figures accumulate like sock fluff have all been faithfully and scholarly retained. English is a brutally gang-raped, bastard language after all.

And so the discourse begins.

- **exercise 1** -

Watch two solid hours of any black slab channel playing videos of old songs (preferably from the 1980s).

Consider that you've merely watched a film. Try to explain to someone you've never met before what the film was really saying.

- exercise 2 –

Take two radios, switch them on, find the nearest channel, record them both playing simultaneously. Find the next channel along, repeat. Consider that you've merely listened to a broadcast.

Try to explain to someone you've never met before, what the broadcast was really about. What does it mean to act?

Act 13: Love and Happiness (reprise)

Kev was looking again at Michelle's Circuit page. She says 'cinema' instead of 'movies'. This is important. Kev's local off-licence had started stocking red and black Oranjeboom at 8.5%. His fourth can was open, in his hand; drinking and looking at Michelle's photos. She says cinema rather than going to the movies. Where had she been today? Kev had walked past her desk three times over the course of the day and not once had he seen her.

His favourite photo of Michelle was the one in the pub with Michelle looking back over her shoulder. Kind of as Nastassia Kinski at the end of Paris, Texas Kev thought, imagining the moment when he would say that to Michelle; the light of recognition seeming to illuminate her whole person. Why had she overlooked him for so long, she'd wonder? What would come after that moment, though, Kev was less certain about. He wished he'd bought six cans from the shop instead of merely the four; trying to decide whether he could be bothered going back for another couple. He concluded that he could. What did he care what the woman in the shop thought of him. Of course he liked that photograph.

The introduction of the significant object of the chair into the text at the point calculated to prove most effective

Blue-cushioned; hand-operated pump system to increase support in lumbar region; numerous previous owners; swivels.

Striped; wing-backed; last significant purchase of a man who would die housing three different types of cancer in his body.

Wooden and with three legs.

Rocks (although rocking to excess could result in compromises to integrity of structure); stains of obscure origins; last seen in a garage in Newton le Willows.

Offering great views of the surrounding bar area; a bugger to get down from.

Class and/or geographical differences possibly accounting for lack of agreement in referencing.

Hanging suspended; feeling as a participant in a vintage soft-porn movie with vague artistic ambitions.

Concrete; open to the elements; lack of exclusivity an important selling point/a not-insignificant drawback; vigilance necessary in avoiding copious splatterings of pigeon shit.

Cushions with a life of their own; the in-laws.

A cloth sack filled with polystyrene beads.

Black Keys

It 'depicts the pair attempting to move a piano up a large flight of steps' and is '"culturally, historically, or aesthetically significant."'

42: iv

i an i: Herr Professor Llavery, Attorney Hassall and Richard, I hope this finds you well. Apologies for not having been in touch, but the house burned down and my head was in those bins over there again. Mendelssohn is re-writing the bible in a materialist sense, he has signed a contract, it is now due in five months. While speaking to Hassall, a suggestion arose that I could feed the facts to you, and that you might write up his stalled biographical material as a tasteful fiction. If we go ahead, we should of course have an agreed procedure in order for the work to be simply processed.

Llavery: 'I was indeed aware of the incident concerning fire. I caught sight of a headline with the words "naked lecturer" and "Mendelssohn" emblazoned together, and it fanned my curiosity. The whole thing seemed so apocalyptic, like the end of Eliot's The Waste Land, the fire sermon. His face was so blackened that if I hadn't been aware of the episode, I would have worried about the racist overtones of the images printed so shamelessly in the newspaper. I fear they exploited the melancholia of that young Germanist Mendlessohn in advance, in fact did they predict it? I of course had imagined Mendelssohn somewhat differently, as an Artaudian actor signalling through the flames on that rooftop in the dark night. I would be delighted to assist you in working through the annus horriblis. How could one ever refuse a publisher called Repeater?

i an i: Herr Ell, I shall, then, send you the bare bones in chronological order, like skeletal bass and drum structures for you to riff on like Anthony Braxton in 1975. Mendelssohn has provided all of these. I shall take the role of Lee Perry, drooling behind the glass and reassembling the fragments, gesamtkunstwerk as scraps. But how do we deal with the inevitable confessional form? Might you take priestly pseudonyms for the business?

Attorney: 'May I suggest we follow Aquinas with the essential "Ego te absolvo a peccatis tuis, in nomine Patris" and "et Filii, et Spiritus Sancti"? The setting would be essential, but rather than it be conducted in some sort of enclosed box, we could conduct it in a sort of peep show booth, or "glory hole". We would all, of course, have to black up for the ritual. We must mum Mendelssohn. Search your conscience deeply until a right way becomes clear. This said, it is becoming clear to me, juridically speaking, that the claim Mendelssohn makes on his own story is possibly no longer valid.

Llavery: 'With some patronising noblesse oblige, I must say that I find your concern touching, perhaps even a little fey. My only role in the confessional would be to dismiss it through laughter. I always preferred to burn my bridges, in the same way that Mendelssohn somehow desired, like the Freudian father who wakes as the candle burns his dead child, to burn down his own self in an act of psychic re-wiring. The violence of telekinesis. Mendelssohn as scanner.'

Attorney: 'I am delighted to hear that we are unified in this endeavour. I should however point out that any possibility of entertaining notions of catharsis and redemption are futile. I would, though, like to say that although I despised Mendelssohn's external circumstances during this ill-fated period, I am utterly prepared to laugh like a drain, again and again.

I, of course desire no increase in profit other than as the process might lead to an exultation of body, mind and soul. I must insist on having full access to, not only the sordid details of all encounters during 2014 and around, but also to the charred remains of the rooftop incident. Let the rooftop speak, let the rooms be bare. Furniture should be moved away from skirting boards. Carpets should be cleaned and vacuumed. The vacuum bag should be emptied and the contents forensically examined. Children should be kept away. We will also, of course, need access to Mendelssohn's bank and credit card records.'

i an i: Agreed. Your first set of Facts will be sent soon and I shall refer henceforth to what I send by this name. This name of Facts. However, it is worth asking, if Mendelssohn were to take another name, a magical name, what would it be?

Editor: 'Might I suggest, in self-loathing, that given your increasing fascination with magic, why not Steve

Handsome? It would add a pleasingly ironic tone.'

i an i: How about Hanke, as in Hanky? With its connotations of tears, melodrama, mucus, semen and masturbation? It could also be shortened to 'Hank', which has connotations of backwoodsmen, Country and Western, as well as the verb to 'pull'... or perhaps even 'Haneke', to flatten signifiers further and raze the significatory ground to ash to smear onto our sweating faces in order to begin the mumming.

Attorney: 'Hanky Panky?'

i an i: Actually, I wish you two would stop messing around and just do some work. Here are your first Facts to process:

'Mendelssohn went to Cupid. Via Cupid he communicated with some women, about ten. Rose answered, she had a green light that told him that she replied often. He talked to Rose. He then got a message from another woman in Hebden Bridge with a canal barge, who was moving off the barge into a house and

trying to sell the boat. He found her more than a little annoying. He went out for a date with Rose. They got very drunk, went back to hers, clothes off, bed. He woke up in Levenshulme. He didn't really know where he was, but he was into city walking at that point, and so walked back to Manchester from there, which was eye-opening. He then lived with Rose and her children for a year and a half. It is worth noting here that Mendelssohn has psychoanalysis notes regarding this period which can be provided upon request. Eventually they split up. Initially Mendelssohn vowed to be single forever, but the itching started, the urges, the rising sense that he was 42 now and only had a finite amount of that sort of thing left in him. He went back to Cupid.' Please respond.

(The rest of this dialogue, pages of it, appear to have been shredded and placed in empty A4 copier boxes. Mouse droppings can be seen in some of these boxes).

Act 14: America

Remembering to shout 'digression' as the speaker goes off topic. The rules of the debating class as recounted by HC, hero of every misunderstood teen which every teen is. As Caulfield, though, I like the digressions and hearing people inhabit them, carried away talking about the stuff that they're into.

Eating slices of pizza as my Harley Davidson cuts up the landscape of my dreams that is America. Eating slices of pizza for my tea every night as cooking, that basic mainstay of adult life, continues thusly something that holds no interest for me and so, if you should ever want me for anything, merely on the off-chance, I mean, come and find me in the freezer section of Tesco after work.

The digression being the key to my poetics, such as they are.

This Saturday morning, for instance, black slab images of George Michael in the corner of the room singing about careless whispers, wondering how I can take that fact somewhere interesting; wondering where that somewhere interesting might be.

The careless whisper, not as a romantic act, but as an act of mumming. The letting-go of significatory telos. Noise as language and language as noise, the whole purpose being the trance state...

That feeling I inhabit, after watching old pop videos for hours on end that the sum of them amounts to something much more important than the individual parts which they, however, possess, still, far from negligible levels of importance. How close I feel to grasping... something. How fed up with myself I feel for my contravention of what I take thusly 'the spirit' of pop. What are the recorded instances of the oldies music channels inducing spiritual experiences in people?

Act 15: The newly present spiritual (England)

Dan Leno and the knocking on the table: We can hardly call the spitting, bacon frying 78rpm shellac he explains this through as 'pop'. Only as in 'snap and crackle'. The desperate needed to know if 'anybody was there', right at the moment when it was becoming vaguely understood that there was not and never had been.

Only the other poor desperados around the card table were 'there', if you can call it that. The supercollider at Cern has now proven that there is nobody there, beyond any doubt. All those millions spent to tell us something about nothing. But it has not yet disproved George Michael's whispers, for his (present tense) is definitely a new present religion.

Give me that new present religion,

It's good enough for me.

Makes me love everybody,

It's good enough for me.

Act 16:

But let us never return to the lie that this place is heaven and hell is for after. I remember that day. There's a Rosé wine bottle by the place that hires out JCBs. Tucked in behind the lamppost by the entrance. Three Quarters full. I thought it might be a tippler at the firm coming out for a smoke, with a drink problem. But Rosé seems a strange tipple, a peculiar choice of drink in a place that seems entirely staffed by men. I am told later that a woman who lives in the street is a chronic alcoholic, 'that'll be hers'.

Stories follow of her 'getting nasty' when asking to borrow money from people down at the Post Office. She sounds as though she is completely unable to quit, drying out consequently bingeing. She is very clever, but her husband is trying to stop her from drinking. She's dried out dozens of times and has been in trouble with the police for going round the houses asking for money. She can turn sour and demand it, one time at the post office a pensioner, she snatched for her bag. A passer-by intervened and no more was made of it.

Act 17: several years ago; ie: THE PAST

Again she shouted out. Had been doing so throughout the lecture. No sense that she might be inhibiting, on the nerves of her fellow students or of the lecturer. Shouting out stuff which was always relevant, sort of; always funny, she believed. A girl known for being funny and always up for a laugh. Do you have something to say, the man at the front of the room, perhaps only ten years older than the girl, asked her; if so, perhaps you'd like to come out to the front and share it with all of us? And instead of shutting up, as probably anyone else would have done, the girl got to her feet and moved herself from behind her desk; at which point, the other students present, most of whom had been doing their best to ignore the girl up to then, began to take notice and to pay attention to what was going on. The girl walked to the front of the room to stand beside the man who'd invited her down. The girl walked to the front of the room and the boy she had merely passed, on her way, cringed for the girl, something the girl didn't notice. What is up with her, the boy thought to himself; why is she always going on with herself like this? And though the girl could read minds her attention was focused elsewhere at that point, she was concentrating on how she would, very shortly, have the room in stitches when she found herself down there, stood beside the lecturer, and so she didn't pick up on the thought she'd merely walked through. Of course though, the girl's plans didn't go the way she'd intended and she failed to notice that what laughter there was in the room was entirely aimed at her rather than taking place with her. The girl's friend, though, sat next to the now empty seat, she wasn't finding anything of what was happening funny. The friend considered what to do.

Upton Speaks

'...that worried reference to stable categories that gave us the title of the ICA London exhibition Between Poetry and Painting in the mid 1960s is still with us. Where am I? How do I behave here? What are the rules?'

Act 18:

Studio apartment or bedsit or single room and kitchen in a converted house in South Manchester.

Lonely and miserable and drinking heavily and eating takeaways.

I got into poetry due to needing to express myself, because I believed in the power of my words to change sensibilities, because I had nothing else to do, because I wanted to go along to the poetry group

I'd picked up a flier for in the hoping of meeting some people and needed something to take with me, because I wanted to be rich, because I wanted to be famous and recognized whenever I closed the door of my studio apartment or bedsit or single room behind me and to be lauded by the general public.

In winter it was freezing there. The window didn't properly meet the frame.

I'd walk to the garage and buy pornographic magazines and masturbate half-heartedly. I had a small pile of them under my single bed.

The wind in the tree outside the window sounded eerie at night. During the day, at weekends, I'd watch the squirrels run up and down the trunk and along the branches.

I'd buy a newspaper and sit on my own in the Wetherspoons reading it hoping someone would approach me to talk, no one ever did.

Everyone needs to express themselves. You can go

nuts if you're denied the means of expression.

My soul.

My soul.

I'd think about my soul and I'd write a poem.

The first poem I tried very hard to make good was about bricks and concrete being all that was visible to one vaguely drawn, unspecific 'I', which – though never expressly stated – was an 'I' based on myself. The poem came about due to the lifetime I'd spent wondering how growing up in a rundown urban environment affected ones aesthetic sense. I felt satisfied with how I'd expressed myself within its lines, I believed in the potential to change subjectivities contained within the poem, I took it along to the group at central library, I felt sure the writing of it would lead very soon to great wealth beyond my wildest dreams, I felt a sense of recognition when I looked in the mirror, I got the poem published in a magazine.

I met some people and wrote some more poems.

And some more poems

and some more poems

and some more.

I began to feel more in control of what I was doing, and trying to do, when I'd sit down to write a poem.

Some of my poems are sexually explicit and some people think that I am writing poems with the express purpose of trying to appeal to men, which is a suggestion I refute. I write what I want to write.

I gave up pornography and started having sex with my partner.

I write as a person trying to appeal to other persons.

I deny men. I deny women.

The Spinster

'A Yewtree Margaret, marginalised, 1957, there are others here, bluestockings the regeneration of the tweeds on dusty posts... Kathleen, the genius, at

Castlefield, the POST fence mother between precocious Britons and the other names, the science names: Rutherford, bluestockings, non-conformists; we revisit to such a degree that you are significant today, growing, inspiring...'

Appendix:

How I got out of poetry, by Tilda Swinton

I got sad and scratchy. Hand-held. On the fly across rubbish dumps and townhouses. On fire. Internally; burning up with the necessity of doing it now and doing it right; our art; our explosion in a dressing-up box, carnival procession of film diary and tangential critique for a couple of quid and a couple of days of our time; oh film poem; oh pioneers of 80s Britain; queer as fuck and loving it as I remembered Derek; beautiful, gentle Derek. What he saw in me to ask me to appear in his film. My first. The times back then: outcast and ostracized, which made us only stronger; our merry band. Shakespeare and ancient civilizations. We were making our own myths. Channelling the combined knowledge of everyone who was around in those days into the creation of these new myths – whose time perhaps hasn't even yet come. The memory of my sad hours alone at the writing desk crumbled beneath my fingers. Nothing and more nothing. The solitary time of writing of trying to find the words for my ideas, of trying to find my ideas, to be able to tune in, precisely, to what was happening in my mind and in my body: it all felt so evil and pointless.

I didn't feel like doing it anymore. I had better things to do. I felt overwhelmed by the success of my debut collection 'short haired and ginger, in the heather' and its follow-up 'box of stillness, box of anger' and seemed unable to any longer live up to my own standards. When I did try to write, on the odd occasion that I would, my words seemed bloodless and unconvincing. I soon gave-up trying.

Everyone was dying: Derek, Richard's dad. There was too much death around. Experimental poetry had seemed to me the forerunner of all future handheld, selfie culture, inspiration for anyone with the energy and at least half an idea to fuck the flag; an unfurled unspread union jack; fuck on it and fuck it; the flag's red, white and junkyard blue where we fuck, me and you, where we fuck to forget the country, the world, its state, it's evil mistress: Maggie beast; Super 8... the ideal vehicle for addressing all this sadness and death and such like: short, fragmented, splintered sections of words able to capture – perfectly – the subjectivity and perceptions of one in mourning. The subtle and fleeting alterations of mood of one in an extreme emotional state... A wonderful match for a high-modernist mode of poetic expression, seemingly. And perhaps I was right; perhaps my initial instincts weren't that far off the mark; however, when I had this additional idea that writing might help me; might help me, by getting everything off my chest and down on paper, get through things; clear my head. Things were just too painful to think about though. I found nothing came. And then more nothing. And after that parcel of nothing had passed along then came some more.

And I tried to write. I tried very hard indeed.

Death casts a long shadow.

Death reminds one, if a reminder is needed, that the time we have is ever so short and fleeting, that we should make the most of our time.

His dad, Richard's dad, on the mortuary slab; looking like his dad but, simultaneously, at the same time that is, occupying the same moment in time and space I mean, looking very much not like him. The way one can be so confident about something and imagine taking that thing in ones stride yet when the time comes the bottom falls entirely out of your world and you think you can go straight home and open up a word.doc and write it all down, thereby getting it off your chest, so a moment or two and respite from the crying is possible but, of course, things don't work out like that. And when you want to write and think it'd help you realise there's not a cat-in-hells chance.

The title of the poetry book I couldn't write was 'the bitter self-loathing of the Scottish upper-classes'.

I played around with alternate titles thinking that perhaps the title was inhibiting me somewhat, though I was still very much, massively, attached to it, yet nothing helped. And so I returned again and again to the upper classes who hate themselves, disablingly. Though perhaps they don't. Perhaps they're quite satisfied with their lives.

My mate at work lent me a DVD; then another and then a shit-load more.

Who can write poems when there's all this death in the world.

I can't stand the thought of anyone else I know dying. Who can write poems when there are all these films to watch.

Sit in a chair in your house on your own and take a book off the shelf. Read it. Think about it. Have pictures in your head which the words have put there. Think about those pictures. Have a reaction; like, an emotional reaction or an intellectual reaction or something; perhaps both. Then go tell someone about what you read and get nowhere because the other person hasn't read the same thing you read or isn't interested in the thing or doesn't understand the thing or else has some other more pressing thing to do than talk to you about books.

Or else decide what you want to see; go to the counter; give the man behind the counter some money and then sit in a roomful of people watching other people, on a screen, do things which you aren't directly involved in and which enable you to forget about all the death for the duration of their onscreen activities, and which enable you to relax the fuck out instead of stretching your very limited brain power as far as it'll go trying to understand what's going on inside you (in order to get all that stuff down on paper).

More on chairs

Match the females with the chairs.

Explain the motivation leading to each female sitting down upon or rising up from those chairs at THIS PARTICULAR MOMENT.

...before the music stops remove one of the chairs.

Press PAUSE to see who is left standing.

Repeat and repeat and repeat until there's only one female left on one chair.

Michelle.

Explain to thaar dead mother the chain of events that led to those particular females having those particular chairs in their homes.

- **interlude (meanwhile)** –

9m ago Peru's Fujimori asks for forgiveness, thanks Kuczynski for pardon

37m ago India says Pakistan wife of convicted spy, seized her shoes

53m ago Twenty-eight arrests after Venezuela looting, violence

1h ago Bitcoin recovers some losses after its worst week since 2013

Act 19: Melodrama

Saturday night... I walked through people barely able to stand who looked as ghosts... pale sick on the pavement a sign of Christmas as much as the usual decorations, fancy dress and noise.

Heading home to the huge white slab, to the huge black slab in the corner. Always on, except for the moments when it isn't. Messages to my brain causing me to remember stuff that means absolutely nothing and has no effect on me at all. I remember this stuff and I feel neither warm nor cold merely… nothing.

In a few days, or a week maybe, anyway at some future present these messages of tonight will cause words to travels to my mouth which will consequently spill out in the air ending up, eventually, in the ears of someone else. Perhaps.

In the bedroom you sleep.

The lights on the tree are off.

Upton Speaks

'We are always terribly courteous to each other. Courtesy may be a large part of it. One learns to hear as others hear.'

Act 20: Three Thousand Word Tragedies x28

'My mother is a huge fan of science fiction, so any black slab I had watched as a child heavily revolved around this theme. On occasion, Metropolis would show itself

on-screen, and each time my mother would talk about how amazing the film was due to its influence on later science fiction. She told me that it doesn't matter if it's black-and-white and has no sound, because that's wha' makes it wha' it is.'

In paraphrasing his mother it should be properly referenced of course. And 'amazing' should have been acknowledged as an authorial emphasis. 'Because that's wha' makes it wha' it is' contains glimmers of a future fusion of semiotics and phenomenology.

This year, all the half-decent writing I was given to mark was massively under word count. But this one was three times the length. I suspect late night submission and course leader filtering. Here is a statement from a future professor of modernism:

'"People like gold," says Dr Alfred Weidinger, one of the foremost experts on Klimt. "It is this metallic aspect that people are attracted to."'

There are perhaps poetic inroads to the borderlines

between enlightenment and alchemy here:

'It was suggested that it was linked or inspired by Einstein's theory of relatively (sic) when asked Dal' said that it was not in fact inspired by this but instead "by Dali's own admission they were inspired by hallucinations after eating Camembert cheese."'

At this point I have started making songs up in my head. All of them are based on Eleanor Rigby by The Beatles: 'Byrony Stebbings, your essay was shit and you know it has been. Lives in a dree-eam. Microsoft windows, crashed on the day you were due to hand-in. Nobody wins. All the rubbish essays, where do they all come from? All the confused ideas, where do they all belong?'

My arse hurts. A lot. That is because I HAVE BEEN SITTING ON THIS CHAIR LOOKING AT THIS STUFF FOR HOURS TRYING TO WORK OUT what IT EVEN IS. The chair that I brought home with me that new year's day; the twin of the chair I'd been rocking back and forth on the night before, watching that crap film and not drinking as my friends thought that me drinking, right consequently, given the circumstances, would be a big mistake. Do we ever inhabit over anything or do we merely spend our lives trying to manage the effects of certain traumas. From now on, I have three grading bands: 68%, 55%, 10%. Forever. They are the only classifications needed here. Eighteen essays to go. I want to inject drugs into my eyeballs. Maybe all of the Cultural Studies department can jump off the roof at the same time holding hands.

At the same time as marking, I'm downloading caches of journal articles as though I won't ever teach in a university again. I'm coming to the end of tenuous tenure. Groundhog Day for the precarious casualised academic. Frantically connecting to the PDFs and hitting 'Download' before going into 'seek' mode again.

Upton Speaks

'*Some collaborations don't continue either because impractical or insufficiently productive. One keeps trying.*'

- interlude (more on music) –

And the aim of the game on this show is to make thaa dance, make thaa laugh, because that is the essence of life of course. Strap tharsels in.

After that we are going to go to our sponsors, our lovely lovely sponsors who make this show possible. Turn that volume up why dunt thaa?

White Keys

'The piano was hammering glinting note heads into a wall of air.'

- Musil, The Man Without Qualities

Act 21: More Tragedies

Flat descriptive fatalism. One dimensional descriptive fatalism. Things are merely how they are, that's merely how it is, you will have to put up with it. It seems that the Guyaki Indians with their 'bad luck in hunting' have a more chromatic mythological system, geared to explaining their circumstances, than the northern post-industrial tribes.

Here there are the straight up fantasists. What we might call the 'northern bullshitter'. The character from Peter Kay, opening a tent to find Robert De Niro across from him. David Wilkinson and I first started discussing this in 2011: They are not fictions. Bradford. A man stuck his head round the door and claimed that his father invented the black slab on Buttershaw Estate, in 1974. Trevor. Playing football with the Happy Mondays and Red Hot Chilli Peppers outside the Apollo in Ardwick. The other guy. The Britart liar. 'I know Damien Hirst' and 'I climbed into the factory with him where we saw the boxes of pharmaceuticals' and this is why I am more than a person working in a bar.

Consequently there's what we might call 'the brotherly love former pill-head bullshitter.' The seething well of aggression operating through 'eh up 'ow are yer matey get on one brother man...'

What he is really saying is 'hang out with me and pretend to like me or I will put you in the hospital'.

Abject = bullshit. It's an equation. Constricted lives mean recourse to fantasy, to escape. We can see it in lite form on the left. Let's all wear hats and retro rucksacks like we're going up a mountain in 1931 and talk loudly of what they taught us about Situationism in class today. Consequently we'll change into tie and shoes and enter the mental rapecamp of real life no better equipped. You can see it in their media. SWP, Stand Up, Spiked, that dreadful article by Sarah Badcock in The Jacobin on the Russian peasants in the revolution, the leftwing adult colouring books of the real hard left which include Stalinist apologia, of which Labour Left are not shy, actually. That's merely off the top of my head, a little while to reckon back would yield lots more. I assume by coming at the last line like that you reckon 'The Left' is one homogeneous blob of ideologically agreed clones marching under red flags to the spaceships to colonise Mars? Thankfully it isn't the case. But we do have two poles here: A flat, dead descriptive fatalism; and a powerful almost hallucinatory ability to fantasise: 'Bundesbank says no euro zone cryptocurrency in sight'. Neat line, when it's all cryptocurrency now.

I am pro Corbyn but not as the Manchester Spring 1917 nostalgios are. What that tells me is that there is a hard core of those people and a whole flabby lot of soft fruit around the hard seed, made of very different, more decomposable stuff, for whom Corbyn means very different things, and this tells me the fruit will partly be eaten and some of it discarded and the seed will have to go in the ground again.

The state is the underwriter of capital, the bailer out of the banks, the giver of coersion, it provides the whip hand of the industries in Job Centres. After 2008 we have no moral duty to any of this. We had no moral duty to any of it before 2008, but after 2008 it is clear. After 2008 we have no moral duties to 'The Nation'. For where is it written? On scraps that don't add up to a constitution. Drop the responsibility, let go the steering wheel, let new social relations emerge from that.

But the neopositivists are substituting 'nation' for 'Party' and by doing this they are returning to Nation. A new moment is the limit of what we can expect: The head of the geist is the anecdote about the man by Newton's grave from the other anecdote - shouting at the hippies about sending a man to the moon via Newtonian physics.

The head of the geist, slightly less whiffy maths than before. Our systems of human equivalence: Language; money.

But language also means red shift as an equivalence. Wooden children's building blocks standing in for the most staggering of concepts, territories and presents. Language means the reduction of all that to scree.

The world is infinite, granular, scalar, focus in and keep going forever, focus out and keep going forever, but language is 8-bit, atonal Eeyore honking: 'We need to unite.' 'Revolving doors.' 'Humanity.' 'Thing of the past.' 'Costs lives.'

The cliche pileup. The only work it does is to pay those who pile it all up in the middle of the motorway, tailbacks causing delays of days and days. The rest of us? We do other work. And try to avoid the pileup as best we can. Take the B, C, D and Z Roads. Offworld Chat.

The young are jubilant and singing, 'oh Je...' The upward curve is definitely new-old Labour, but there is a strong sense of how the waning end of that curve is present in the upswing. The alpha and omega are not separate or separable, they are one. The central force of gravity that is pulling the rising, brightly coloured balloon down is the approaching exit from the European Union.

What do all politicians share? A series of governments of different colours have flown their tenure since World War Two on the seat of their pants and on a series of inflated truths, while managing to conceal inconvenient facts. Backs of envelopes, backs of fag packets. Some of them had infrastructural luck. North Sea Oil, for instance. But here lies a submerged potential future struggle. The Scottish Independence narrative has not gone away, it has only gone quiet. A contemporary mirror image can be seen in the current forced alliance of the Conservative Party with the DUP.

New-old Labour will hit the permanent paradox, that a revolution without a baseline reconfiguration of value away from money will always leave it bankrupt: It has to square the circle of being in capitalism while delivering socialism.

London has swollen to the point where it nearly burst. A series of violent and immoral lancings have reduced the sore to a meniscus, but Manchester and similarly scaled cities are now bloating too. This is not to make a xenophobic argument about 'incomers', but one regarding a model of city governance that can only play one game, that of property, culture and economics. It plays that game badly too, failing to tax the local and international moneymakers properly. It plays the game largely for the players.

Agglomeration theory, along with what is known in its quotidien guise as 'trickle down', with its simplistic counterpart of 'connect-up', best seen currently in HS2, HS3 and other new rail links, has been largely disproven as an effective stimulant for an empty economy. Yet Manchester is about to gamble its future all the way up to 2032 on this game plan.

Leese and Burnham have really big fucking train sets in their attics. They go home and sit on the floor in their engine driver caps singing 'choo-woo'.

Saskia Sassen understands how the concept of 'competing cities' undermines stability and disenfranchises ordinary people. But this is exactly what Manchester is becoming. There are all kinds of cultural assumptions around how 'we' must prove ourselves to Westminster. They are not officially scripted in policy, but are evidence of a continuing masculine managerial culture, a hangover from industrialism and the puritan work ethic. Not only that, but 'the city' has signed up to a berserk, sadomasochistic deal with central government, a 'cash back' deal which, if it becomes the default model of city governance in the UK, will further Americanise urban Britain. This could create a winners-and-losers culture at the macroeconomic level.

Oh Jesus. The 'we'. 'We' should, 'we are', we...

Just get religion and have done with it you tossers.

Dub 2:

Inhabit to dimensional fucking gas, not dimensional as in 'only Korea Disney means the tenure, "the education"', an everyone happy copious social. The freezer preserving the Rosé missile. Competition on me is me, my videos, thar home, thar going central from us neo-Beatles, who decide the prison pavement, pious fuck. This lot don't game classifications for Eeyore. Abject police time is due. Weidinger Ardwick and the chromatic Mercedes. A social heavy blob completely puffed with wonder. A surprise act, yet prescriptions were filled.

- note to reader -

Apart from to say 'don't look for continuity why would you' there isn't one.

The Spinster

'We make worthy RUMINATIONS, archaeologies only see SOME jagged layers, nonetheless, not to be caricatured, trumpet women, much of Byzantium is fitting of genderless, gorgeous museum, numerous of the good at the figures, the double-ledger, the women that schoolgirl became, the list dedicated to the infamous portrayal...'

42 v

Mendelssohn and eye contact. His gaze remaining fixedly to the side, above or below; appraising the decoration around my fireplace perhaps, the crayon drawings of my children, my certification of professional competence awarded in glittering ceremony and pomp; my visage avoided at all costs. Puts his head down in the street when girls pass, puts his head down in the street when girls pass.

Upon first entering my consulting room, my outstretched hand and invitation to proceed, hugging the threshold, eyes briefly glimpsed and oh what lovely eyes they are: so accepting yet enquiring; proud yet humble; experienced yet innocent; blue yet grey yet green. The eyes of Mendelssohn the windows of his bungalow, permanently shuttered by his downcast, raised or sideward glance. Does he feel himself alone during our sessions? Is his imagined solitude a necessary condition of his speech, his disclosure? How his determined refusal to look at me impacts upon my own sense of personhood. But then this is not about me…

The frequency of his tales of irritation on public transport and in cinemas. Behind him teenagers on phones and infants squawking; the intrusion into his thoughts and concentration of all the everyday noise of the world; the impossibility of avoiding such noise as a person existing in the world. The angry glances cast over his shoulder; the death stares maintained for the entirety of the leg between White City (PC World) and the church towards the end of Chester Road. His ease and readiness to attempt eye contact with strangers, eyes contact loaded with meaning and intention (shut-up; vacate my space; alter your entire mode of existence) and, yet, the difficulty he has meeting the gaze of people (myself) that he has built up this professional relationship with over this number of weeks. Which, of course, is no contradiction at all.

And then to his thoughts… the constant return to his ambivalence regarding the primary caregiver triangle which was rendering analysis opaque, or even, I have to use the word, impotent.

The thought he has spent the intervening years berating himself for due to, as he puts it – the qualifications ever present, though – its inappropriate nature which, he knows, oh yes he knows!, was entirely understandable due to his age but, nevertheless... The statement about not blaming himself undercut by the overpowering sense of blame accompanying the expression of such statements. Necessity of encouraging him to be kinder to himself. To lower, somewhat, the exacting standards of behaviour he imposes upon himself. Of course though he says, as he would, that he needs his standards for how else could he effect change in his life if it wasn't for such standards. How his constant striving to achieve some illusory standard of being impacts upon his equilibrium. My frequent interjections to point out to him that that was his critical self that spoke, not him, and that he needs to encourage the corner of his brain that has taken on the role of critic to relax, take it easy, put their feet up for a while. His angry and focused stare, in response, deep into the subterranean hidden depths of my carpet.

The process of putting oneself up for sale in the pursuit of amour; primped and preened in multi-coloured shirts which never used to concern me but now it's making me sick; nevertheless, the need of rejoining the dance; of stepping one more time upon the floor, heart light with hope, feet heavy with anticipated failure. The dance, the dance, the push and the pull… Persistent memory of the encounter with the mysterious stranger in the long black coat and strong aroma on Princess Road, just lately stepped off the Hulme Bridge as he stated, keen to pass on to me an unbowdlerized account of certain of the events of his forty second year; hoping, I understood, to inspire me to similar heights myself; but no! all advice was unwanted that night as I sped euphorically on; how I could ascend higher than the peak I currently occupied was a question which troubled me not, all awareness of any heights further to climb lost to me. With my head to the sky I continued on; lost to my thoughts – my precious thoughts!; missing the concrete skeleton of the unfinished future apartment block facing First Street, construction halted indefinitely awaiting a further injection of recalcitrant dough; blindly stumbling through the assorted ghosts of past radicals still haunting the now built over site of so many anti-Tory meetings of years gone by; deaf to their hoarse pleas that I purchase a copy of their newspaper . . .

A state fated not to last however – sadly, predictably – and once more I would soon begin to see my surroundings; begin to remember where I was, in which room, in which city . . '

His vulnerability so clearly apparent through the regular complaints regarding his partner's behaviour; the repetitively inevitable disappointment that the way he is being loved seems to him to fall short of the way he would like, in his night-time mental wanderings, to receive that love. Connections that he, himself, seems absolutely aware of; connections, too, between the exacting standards he has regarding his own behaviour and the same, similarly high standards he seems to have of his partner, particularly in respect of the way she chooses to parcel up and distribute to him her love. The inner critic. The constant vigilance of that part of his brain observing and noting and measuring all of his words and actions. Remarks of said critic in my consulting rooms. An unguarded moment when he seems to be finally communicating meaningfully, only to be swept aside by some affected remark or attempt at humour. For all that he often seems to imagine me out of the room I sometimes have the sense that he isn't present himself: that it's some actor playing a part sat across from me rather than a real human being.

Black Keys

'In which Laurel and Hardy are midwives, but keep getting distracted by having to carry a piano upstairs, with hilarious consequences.'

Act 22: towards a taxonomy of enjoyment

Not long into my run through of Michael Haneke's filmography, merely after Benny's Video, I think it was, I suffer the unexpected descent of the old, familiar sense of hopelessness that has been with me, on and off, most of my life. I don't help myself, she says; asking me why I've decided to watch every film Haneke has made. I merely want to watch them, I tell her; choosing not to say more about my motivation, though feeling I could. I am called a fool and my recent decision to reduce the dosage of my citalopram is brought up, again. It'll pass, I say, meaning my mood; thinking, whilst I'm saying as much, of the next Haneke film on the list that I'm looking forward to watching the following evening.

With their graphic scenes of violence and brutality I wonder what it means to say I enjoy a Michael Haneke film?

What is the nature of that enjoyment? In what does it consist?

Perhaps I might consider other occasions when I could say I enjoyed myself, occasions which would perhaps be more widely understood as being enjoyable . . . what can I learn about my feelings for Haneke's work from such considerations? What does it mean to act?

Saga 0

Saga 'is a revival of the tragic genre in the age of the abject. This has been initiated as a proposal by Hhassall, Llavery and Rraves. It is the product, 'worked in', of the forty-twos. The latter also inhabits the text – to a greater or lesser degree – and in this he shadows the compositional strategies, as both author, trope, and collection of rain-soaked, compounded receipts in the gutter, by the iron drain covering.'

- interlude -

A much-celebrated gannet, the only one of its kind living on an island off the coast of New Zealand, has been found dead surrounded by concrete replicas of birds it is believed he thought were his friends and family... His body was found alongside one particular concrete gannet replica conservationists say he believed was his partner. [The gannet] had attempted to woo the replica in 2013 in an act of courtship, which led to him building a nest from seaweed, mud and twigs for the bird... wildlife officials first placed the concrete replicas on the cliff side in December 1997... in hopes of establishing a new colony..."

- Independent online, Feb 3, 2017

105

Act 23: Stockport post depot

A guy with a huge long Mercedes tries to park, in out, in out. He is blocking the entrance to the car park. The long queue waiting to collect their post are all looking. It's a cold day but the doors are wedged open. I eventually sigh and go round the side and lock my bike up. I join the queue. They are all discussing how he has been trying to park for at least ten minutes, fifteen in one estimate. He consequently tries to reverse into the space where my bike is parked and I have to go out to check he doesn't hit it. He doesn't, but he leaves the front end of the car sticking right out. 'Maybe he can get a longer car' I say. Nobody laughs. He comes inside to join the queue and absolute silence follows. I pick up my post. Out the front is a sign that says 'avoid reading whilst walking'.

Saga 1

Rraves: 'Gobert Rraves should be given his own pamphlet soon, or beat combo, or both. And it's pronounced Go-bert Rraves, OK? As in go-to, or go-getter, or gobshite. But whatever either of you do - and what would I know about any of that - don't mention any of this to his wife, Gobertina Rravez...'

'Attorney: How did you guess, Rraves... the only one clever or perverse enough to see the latency of the message... The next project is about poison gas, zoos, shit.....'

Rraves: 'The situation, is indeed paramount, as was the mounting of the paras, and likewise the ma-ing of the la's, and the ululating of the You-u-Lore.'

Client: 'Gobertina always maintained (at least to me) that the pronunciation of her name was as in Flaubertina, or Go-betweener, depending on the situation. I remember saying to thar lad 'save us the big bits youth'. You snorted into your ale. Gobert, does

Gobertina know of the devastated Jewish heiress you left sprawling, of the numerous discarded calling card socks, drenched. Does she know of our times on "the balcony", of those wailing banshee custard chucking hecklers? I urge you to consider this.'

The Spinster

'It was and will be BEWILDERED unless some controversial beautiful wonder, some inspirational driver LEARNS Boudicca! The Coming Kingdom links back ANACHRONISM! This is a WARNING!'

Act 24: several years ago; ie: THE PAST

My legs feel weak. I know I'll be able to make it to the cash-point, yet at the same time I wonder if I will or if I'm perhaps going to end up a heap collapsed on the pavement, the early morning commuters passing me by, stepping over me and such like. Actually, is it that my legs feel weak or has the air got suddenly heavier? Each movement of my legs necessary to put one foot in front of the other seems to take such an effort; the air weighing down heavily on me, resisting my moments, pushing back against me. Trying to ride out the panic. This is not something I'm feeling for the first time. It'll pass. It'll pass. Relax, keep walking and get through it. And I do; almost as soon as I realise I'm having difficulty walking the feeling's gone. I'm walking fine. A relief as I must get to work to deal with those numbers.

Saga 2

Attorney: 'Creating chaos, spoiling the fun, destroying things as Reo Speedwagon play gently from the cheap mesh speakers, located in the top right hand corner of the room, facing the huge wide black slab spewing out endless streams of neo-liberal propaganda - the angry box. Rraves thought he was out of it at last, only to find himself inexorably drawn in against his wishes. His unconscious, of course, was delighted. He had started to enjoy his symptom.'

Rraves: 'One must write the symptom, then cloak it, in the shape of letters made of cranes' legs... You know this Attorney, you know this all too well... Take some advice from Rraves - the ritualistic knicker, the stalkermind, the next door mining - all keep one out from shadows of all kinds, the light is harsh there, but it is clear.'

Attorney: 'My memories - if memories they are - of Gobertina concern the day she left us... you had just finished mainlining bleach into your eyeball when she appeared doe-eyed and listless in the pit we called the sitting room. The violence of her vulnerability was provocative... both of us had to shield ourselves from its scorch... I remain haunted by her shadow.'

Rant 1

NEVER POSITIVE NEVER FROM EITHER OF THEM YOU MUST TRANSFER YOURSELF AGAINST THIS

I was talking to someone I used to know, she said she'd moved to London and I said I don't envy you, the rents, etc. I saw she'd 'bought a house' but worked in Starbucks, at 21. The double-barrel name, the frocks, money. I get the *FT*. To check what's going on. Alleyne on indexes. *How to Spend It*. Three bed flat 4.6 million. She didn't reply. This is the real class divide and I don't align myself with the buyer campaigner it is conservative and self-seeking. But with pension funds in crisis, the welfare state ripped up, the owners have a future and wealth, the rest have the ghetto. There is nothing about any of this that is more natural or benign than the rule of The Pharoahs. And that silence at the end the conversation, the class divide that dare not speak its name, because it is no longer spoiled brats wanting more complaining about those who have even more - the privileged and those in dire peril is all.

ALWAYS A SIGH ALWAYS ABOUT ANYTHING I DO, IN THE FACE OF WHICH NEVER EVER GIVE CREEDENCE TO ANYTHING THEY EVER SAY OR DO AND AIM FOR OUT AND INDEPENDENT BUT STACK AWAY CASH STOP BUYING RIGHT NOW - HOUSE - TINY HOUSE TINY HOUSE GOD PLEASE

I have done quit booze become a doctor book out paper out in journal new book contract - why would anyone throw that away for a supermarket job, it's crazy! She understood that - encouraging me to go when it made no money for a year - all my friends understand that - what you have to understand is how exceptional all this is.

HERE MILE RADIUS LIKE MOORE PREACH AMONG YOUR PEOPLE JOHAN YE OUT THE WHALE BELLY

A sighs and B aggressively says 'do you get charged?' 'Does it pay?' You can only advise me to do what you understand and I need advice on things beyond your understanding. It isn't wrong you don't know about this stuff why would you? But what is wrong is that you actively try to advise me to stop doing it. It's very draining. Having to do this, having to justify my existence.

Y WAS TELLING ME TO COME BACK WITH THE FIRE, GEOGRAPHICALLY, AWAY FROM THIS ZONE BUT ALSO IN TERMS OF MY ACTION - WRONG PATH – With or against traffic.

Internal echo of 80s chart hit existentialism thinking perhaps the time has come to buy a used car during this time of funerals and death reminiscences. Fuck your hand-sanitizing, finger drumming table-top, desk bullshit for what it is: a waste. Sad, distressing waste of a life in number shuffling, ra-ra skirt wearing 80s pop moves. I can't dance. There is a poem that says as much, says something about something else involving words and deliberate narrative fragmentation. I check my bank balance and I am alarmed in feelings and in an unexpected raise in temperature…

BUT ALSO PREACHING IN YOUR OWN LAND IT IS JONAH I BACKED AWAY FROM MY DUTIES BUT NOW I AM BACK ON THEM AND WILL NOT STOP. Y, SPEAK TO ME

Act 25: several years ago; ie: THE PAST

The doc said he was prescribing me sertraline due to the two suicide attempts in my past; said if it hadn't been for those he probably would have tried to avoid medication; said he thought my feelings were to be expected given the circumstances. "I'd like to thank my dad, who's dead; and everybody else, who isn't".

Was a terrible drug for me though: no sleep; no food and a broken knob.

Of course there'll be side effects the doctor had said; they'll last for a few weeks but, eventually, they'll pass; just try to ride the side effects out.

And when I described those side effects to a different doctor, a month or so later, he – immediately – asked me why on earth I was still persevering with Sertraline; why I hadn't stopped taking it straightaway. Well, the side-effects, I told him… the other doctor said… Come off it. You mean wean myself off it? I asked; imagining the drama of the deleted scene from *Trainspotting* as I, racked with sweats and sickness, tried to beat my overwhelming craving for the drug. No, the doctor said; just stop taking it. And when you go through reception on your way out make another appointment with me for a couple of weeks time and we'll try you on something else.

Saga 3

Rraves: 'Gobertina knows of all of this. She knew of it even as the calipers bit and Little Goberta splobbed forth. An interesting caveat to all of this is that I, The Go-bert Rraves, considered the story of The Jewess to be bunk, even as I left her sprawling and ventured back into the snow, or perhaps to go next door to feel up the frigid church organist, but no, I have now seen pictures of her coming though customs with Daddy and Twiggy, en route to the McCartneys, in 1974. All of this was occulted into the future of 2052, by inhaling deeply on her post-coital Marks and Spencer panties full of whisky - pack of four for eight pounds - Christmas 2010-11, from where it now feeds back into the present. The single most frightening thing about all of this, Dear Gentlemen, is just how little of this discourse is now fictional.'

Attorney: 'Dear Rraves, Is she still interested in liberation theology? Her days in Colombia must have brought her into contacts with the Jesuits of Santa Cruz... Did you bury the Panda live? My god... it was what, so big... and I remember the badger baiting with fondness. You in the twilight covered in blood, and laughing about the drought. Are you still gassing animals in the name of science, Go-bert? And does your wife still have that delightful Palomino pony?'

Act 26:

The woman at the counter who judges with her face. I'm out and before my script. She is judging. Do you pay for your prescriptions? I say yes and she moves, a signal of grudging acceptance. A sideways glance from another member of staff tells me there are people behind the counter who don't like her either. All the sense of instinct and body language in it. The stuff sociologists usually exclude. And of course those observations and feelings may be totally wrong. But their wrongness is part of the social. So Sociology

- herebefore most of it - which excludes such things is not of the social. They view me through their knee jerk reactions and I through mine. The Sociologist repressing these in the name of enlightenment reason - which is what is going on - are doing the equivalent for the social of the discontent under civilization that Freud understood well. 'Don't trust Sociologists', thus spake The Red Krayola. Right an' all.

Communities, in work or outside, are always already ideological. They always include in order to exclude. They would not be communities if they did not do this. Because if they didn't do this you wouldn't have to mark the 'com' or 'co' in the prefix of the word. Community always already means its opposite too: You have to go to the Companies House documents to get the addresses; 'competition come sideway, competition come straightway.'

The condition of temporariness cuts in from below. If you manage to get 'settled' at 35, 40, 45, you spent an eternal present in unsettled and therefore 'unsettling' conditions and the present and experience leading up to that undermines your state of being 'settled'. You become your cage. But your cage is the unstable vortext.

The always having to explain yourself. Well, you should be into enough things now for 'something to happen', or well it might 'lead to something'. Always from those who don't realise how the laws of life have shifted, because they don't have to live in that bubble of social physics. Things no longer lead to other things unless you lived at a present when they did, and you arrived 'there', on permanent full time with a mortgage and stayed there. It's always already seen as not extreme but its extremity is its liberalism. The saturation depth of liberalism being the extreme, its fundamentalism.

I go thusly and read Zizek. Zizek reads Zizek, redoubles via Hegelian slight of hand, becomes Zizek again, but more than Zizek, Zizek presents Zizek, swollen to encompass all of the land, and sea, and space, and present... I am not of ur world.

Richard Barrett said similar things first. About Kanye West. Richard Barrett says the thing you never nous about saying. He gets there first.

Richard

Steven

Richard

Steven

Richard

Steven

Richard

Steven

Saga 4

Rraves: 'Those were the days Attorney, none of those protests outside the compound, and yes, as you ask, Gobertina spent a lot of time attempting to decode the neo-transfiguration in Santa Cruz, but this is a long time before the baby auctions began, after which she was far too busy, and by then, frankly, she didn't give a tuppenny toss: She is a lady of Yorkshire extractions. We remember you also, laughing at the letters made by the cranes' legs, once the hosing-down was partially underway, and one could see them through the effluent. We stopped gassing animals here in nineteen forty-five. We had a break until fifty-six, then we started burying them alive. My wife no longer has the Palomino pony, but she does have massive badongers. Before your ethical protests begin, 'massive badongers' is her own description. She is also a lady of latin extractions.'

- Yours, Gobert Rraves and Gobertina Rravez.

The Spinster

'*THE deal women, the TRIP ethnographers, archaeological moderns and painters, particular of the pasts, concerning the manchizzle inspiration city, league EXPLORER, her interest seems CONSTANTLY on the myth and reality...*'

Upton Speaks

'*...a moose drunk on autumn berries is to be treated with caution.*'

Dub 3:

The venom scale repetition, the destruction, the dirt-first coffee. Nowheresville next to the sheer novelsworths that are permanently the Little Norway of the imagination. Thaars is dug dead as a blood grave. I am an unrest. Couple up thaar 'no' and don't go as the future losers. Suddenly bag something, inhabit onto things, A to B comprising black slab towel, rightward reckoning individual. Thus influenced thaa go miles and hammer unrest into a soul, left all the words behind in the clampdown. Cut the right cloth. Make the border.

Rant 2

BECAUSE THAT IS SUICIDE

I am: Symptoms -

WORKING TO SCRAPE BY NO WRITING Not in words, the poor medium of words: the horizontals of the letters bending against my bodyweight as I pass, delivering me a sharp thwack in the face. Everything is against me: the traffic, the wind, the rain and all the rest of the weather. I remember everything. My head a constant, non-stop running loop of my entire life from the beginning to now and back again before resuming and seeming to cancel itself out: a copy of a copy of a copy of a copy... Fuzz and disintegration. Snow. Black and white disappearance of subjectivity into the picture's interference up on the screen. Nothing is clear...

OUT OF THE SYMBOLIC ARENA HERE IS VERY REAL DANGER

White Keys

'Clarisse leapt up in mid-chord and banged the piano shut; Walter barely managed to save his fingers.'

- Musil, The Man Without Qualities

42 vi

His expectation of exceptionalism and sense of disappointment at slow, dawning realisation of conformity of type. How everything, for him, comes back to the mother and his initial resistance in accepting that. Though impacting forcefully upon him nevertheless it all seems to have left next to no permanent psychic imprint at all. Talk of the more recent events as screen to avoid having to talk about the earlier; how many weeks was it before the fire was mentioned?

And then the disclosure of the earlier suicide attempts: alcohol and painkillers before, later, multiple lacerations to wrist areas. Shock at that disclose. His general and persistent levels of moroseness not preparing me for those words. His laughter following; dismissive; embarrassed; entirely inappropriate (and yet he gets upset at people, as he puts it 'taking him the wrong way' with, seemingly, no consideration at all to the cues he's providing them with); me questioning him on it, on his laughter, as I do on each such occasion he behaves similarly. 'You understand what a big thing that is you've just told me?' And of course he understands. His understanding knows no bounds.

The idea he wanted to try out then, explore, in the following week's session regarding the pills and the cuts as being ritualised attempts at re-writing the history of Lancashire: a brush with death which proves non-fatal; as though by surviving his self-inflicted wounds he could, somehow, on some level, bring it back to life. What did Burgess say? Death and this region are not one when one prefers death to it.

Letting him speak, get it all off his chest, but my scepticism; my trying to make him see that the very logic of this hypothesis all but proves its erroneousness. The logic of delusion. All I see in it is evidence of his literariness that he never fails, each week, to refer to. Neat; too much so; too tidy. The mother though, all the same, remaining, undeniably, key.

How he goes to pieces when things crop up which cause divergences from his plans and how he thinks that that going to pieces might be some sort of echo of his response to his mother, the first great divergence from a plan to ever impact upon him. How important, always, the plan is in his life, of knowing precisely how each moment of every day is to be accounted for, almost as though a plan is a kind of attempt at controlling fate, keeping its contingencies and chance occurrences at arm's length; the contingencies and chance that another man might welcome. Me needing him to relax; to loosen his hold.

Telling him the difficulty I have in imagining what going through life in such a way must be like, how stressful it must be. Telling him, as well, I think this insight means something, that he's onto something. Asking him to consider, though, in relation to all of this, the question of age; how the fact of him being at mid-life and, consequently, aware of the likely amount of time left to him informs these thoughts of his. After all, we're, each of us, getting older.

The Spinster

'Niblock's books, SPINSTER at the welcome, the anthroslug book... The Museum, many more and more CONTEMPORARY are of the EDWARDIAN short

submarine fencer, an INDUSTRIAL ADVENTURER,
who was anthropological - shamelessly - for of the
female scientifics in the activist ancient Sunday
FLANEUSE, the ambulance social hurts...'

Black Keys

'Is playing the piano normal? It's an unusual state
of excitement associated with tremors in the wrists
and ankles. For a physician, there's no such thing as
normal.'

- Musil, The Man Without Qualities

Rant 3

THE JUDGING THE JUDGEMENT THE NOISES
THROUGH THE FLOOR THE SIMPLISTIC IDEA
OF WHAT PEOPLE SHOULD DO TO GET AHEAD
THE SHEER BLINKEREDNESS THE POURING
INTO OTHER PEOPLE'S LIVES - ABOUT 'HER
JOB SITUATION' - WHICH WAS ME CATHECTED

BACK IN RESENTMENT

Fucking rage

WELL SHE SHOULD JUST GET A SUPERMARKET JOB

Medicated, half medicated. Walking. The photograph's time contained in the over-exposed, darkened ink. Line between two points of future occult, sex magick and the slow decline dryness and heat of winter, past car-showrooms and carpet warehouses. Sand underfoot. Desert theory. Imaginings and visions of 'real price' stickers detailing the exact savings possible when all around here, really, really, I mean when you really think hard about it, is loss only and the memory of that loss… Memory of his twenties, earlier, overlaid like carpet on the most recent picture. Seeming so pointless now. Everything. All of it except the fight to keep the dark stuff at bay by whatever means available. A voluntary reduction of meds. A sickening. Walking, walking backwards, feeling like.

Reverse. Rewinding slowly in a faulty, antique VCR, back to the point of birth and all that blood and body tearing open, apart; for what.

Act 27:

My back aches. I have pulled something or something. My poor back. My move to the higher chair in an attempt to reduce stress on my back when in the act of sitting down and getting up again. The higher chair by the window out of which I now look and notice, first, the car pulling into the carpark beneath me and, then, above us all – above myself and the parking car, the sky, the pale bluey, grey sky with the smudge of clouds, their upper-most edge picked out in bright orangey-yellow. I love the sky, I have always loved the sky. What do I care about anything as long as I can look up and still see the sky above me. It is nearly time for some more Ibuprofen. Perhaps, in a moment, I will use the freeze-spray upon the affect area again.

Act 28: the revolution will depend upon a flexible courier service

When I finally emailed Verso Customer Services department hoping to find out what had happened to the books I'd ordered in their winter sale I was told that the courier had tried to deliver my order but had been unable to.

There was no sign of a note, or similar, in our flat's letter box; no sign of any attempted delivery whatsoever.

I asked Verso if they'd either be able to redeliver the books at a time when I could ensure I'd be at home.

It was impossible to give me notice of the delivery date and time I was told; also, it would be impossible for me to collect the books from a depot used by the courier. In short, there was no way of getting these books to me and so I got my money back and potential comprehensive societal change was averted.

White Keys

'Harold Lloyd and Mildred Davis at the piano, 1935.'

- exercise 3, towards achieving some semblance of narrative coherence –

Take down from the shelf your copy of Constance DeJong's Modern Love plus every Kathy Acker book you own; select your favourite from the pile of Acker books . . . read a page of DeJong and then a page of Acker, a page of DeJong a page of Acker, a page of DeJong and a page of Acker, become possessed by the Divine Spirit of 70s downtown New York and realise all your prejudices and expectations regarding literary fiction are wrong and that you know absolutely nothing. Experience this realization as a liberation. Feel the possibilities. Feel them. Go on, feel them!

The Spinster

'We see the Captain Author, we see HE that belies our greatest Bitch, the matter against the INTREPID and great... you're a gentle person... Post BEING the present case borders on thankless when the LANDSCAPE spirit across generations witches the sabre, and man himself is now UNFASHIONABLE, I say this, of the writer, the Niblock OF bluestockings, the old theme, but quite new work for a linguist...'

Act 29:

The girl stands outside Superdrug, Piccadilly Gardens, Manchester. People passing; trams passing. A bus journey to get her here. Ipod in, the sound of the passengers blocked. This is what The Circuit says; this is what Codex says; she has no idea what Twitter says at this moment in time: half five in the evening, rush hour. Lasting for a span of 2 or 3 hours in this city. Does anyone notice him stood there outside the store.

Checking her phone. The guy is due soon. A couple of texts from him already saying he is on his way. How different will he be in person? The construction of a personality over a series of late night phone-calls and texts. Constructed or else faithfully conveyed. Worries of discrepancies and gaps big enough to die in between the image in her head and the image she's soon going to be confronted with. Kids enter to buy spot cream and hair bands and whatever else kids buy. Durex and energy drinks. Keep looking at the people approaching, trying to notice him. His phone goes again. Coffee.

Coffee with unsuitable woman after unsuitable woman. Mister mistress. Bit on the side but still, something keeps her trying again and again hoping that this time this one might be different and might lead to the one thing he wants, same as the thing everyone wants. Don't say it too soon. Remember not to say it too soon nor to go home with him too soon. She will be in the driving seat. She will play it right this time. He will say you are everything I want but it's too soon for me to stick to these rules that everyone seems to know without anyone once having been formally told them; I won't leave it a number of days before texting you back, she thinks and he thinks as well as he hits send on his phone, again, to say he's just getting off the tram and she'll be able to recognize him as he'll be the one carrying the massive bunch of flowers.

Though is it the one thing everyone wants? The girl neither knows nor cares; he just knows it's the one thing he wants. So sick of being alone or if, when not alone, being with people who couldn't care less about her, really. Knobheads and users. The years spent trying to unpick and untangle her psychology, her upbringing, to figure out why this is so important to her, why she wants it so much. Everyone she knows managed to get settled years ago, an easy, seemingly simple and straightforward process that he's, yet, somehow managed to balls up repeatedly. The lack of a model of a successful adult relationship when growing up posited as a deciding factor in his failure. Dead mother and, now, dead father. The effort to muster sufficient energy to carry on and try again when one thing ends; how pointless all that seems, yet, at the same time, how absolutely the point of everything it all is. Our relationship is the most important thing in my life. Forget all the rest of it; lying here with you, now, is all that matters.

Such words . . . love being impossible to talk about, to analyse; all that there is are the conditions which make words of love possible: how did those two people get to such a situation where one could say to the other that they love that person and the other could have some sense of what those words mean? Trace the routes to such a declaration; forget the words themselves, the content, instead trace back life-stores and personal histories to this room, now, where those words are being exchanged in response to something approaching comprehension.

Black Keys

'He had to say something, and felt like a piano in the fraction of a second between the moment when the ten-fingered crash of an incredible blow hits it and the cry of pain.'

- Musil, The Man Without Qualities

Act 30: Leaving Planet Ex

The two in the grey towelling, the renegade uniform. Walking as Thunderbirds puppets. The strings are more visible, twitched into existence by the gods Neoweed, Alcohol and Smack. They look as they may be puppeteers themselves and well they might be.

Sreet. Chip oyle. Chip oyle arr Lee. Sreet innit. Yer get pea wet ere. The problem with Ex is that everyone in

Ex looks as they're in Ex. The problem Ex 'as is that it's in Ex.

It's inside itsel', an that's inside itsel' an all an its peeple ur inside umsels. It dunt naa it's inside itsen tho'.

The peeple dunt naa they're in it, or in the… They dunt naa there's another thing that people are in. They dunt naa that there's another thing fer peepl tu be in. I 'ate those Russian Dolls, they're so full o' themselves. As people from Zed. Lolz. Fuck um. Sreet. Chip oyle. They were so familiar with each other insults could be thrown all day leaving no marks.

A hole full of jumpers, on Black Friday. Your shopping basket is empty. Let your shopping basket be empty forever. When things fall to the floor they vanish forever, into another realm. An entirely symbolic curtain through which one passes, think of heavy drapes. Think of a slab of heavy tranking daylong provincialism.

Nous up thy reckoning. At least nous up it.

I hear the shrieking. The ethics voice. 'You can't say that.' Although what they are really saying is that you can't say that like that. And what they really mean is you can't say that because only me and my friends can. And if you go in as a Victorian Missionary not only can you say it but you can meddle in actual lives. Well fuck you all who are pulling everyone into the rules of your discourse in order to oversee the policing of that discourse in the name of liberal 'freedom'. The Missionary Position. The most libertarian are the most sharp elbowed, arms with invisible scalpel blades cutting thee to ribbons, leaving thee defenceless. The only hex is this one, showing the blades thus. Or, rather, 'never trust a hippie.'

Our present is the present of the new positive. On both sides of the political break. It may be named the neosolid, or the 'post-ironic' - the most hilarious, naïve, hopeful, and utterly confused new term - but the real underlying philosophical shift is the expulsing of negation. With this understood I run to the opposite. To Horkheimer, Freud and Lacan, the latter two perhaps the most horrific to the neopositivists. All that seething non-rational under the surface. Merely ice it over forever, they almost reckon, but never quite do. Nous up thar reckoning. At least nous it up, right?

White Keys

Pia pia piano, piano, piano

Act 31: Returning to Planet Zed

We need to stop picking up the pieces. So, if there is no communication officer we don't communicate, if there's no treasurer, no money, no work gets done. Sink into the space that opens up and relax in it. Mould it as a comfortable familiar shoe. People don't know how to 'merely live' anymore. They're either eleven hours a day on some exhausting unrewarding crap or retraining to be some other nothing puffed up to sound like something, or doing some bullshit to try whatever... 'finding themselves', be a writer, dancer, musician. Merely live.

The thing to fear the most is the return of a simpler world on the right and left. Why? The naturalisation of work. The naturalisation of money as a transparent signifier of value. The on-off machine, the fort-da game. There-gone, there-gone, there-gone. 1 0 1 0 1 0. Digital, day in day out day in day out. Me and me girlfriend have been together on and off on and off. I inhabit work, on and off. The relationship is binary, but the polite middle class surface sheen covers over that binary with an analog gloss. Underneath lies the infantile punishment-reward of adult and child. It fits into the going order, the division of labour, as a hand into a glove.

The problem is not living frugally, but everyone living as Emperor Nero, over-production, over-consumption. The more you consume the less you live. The more you live through consumption the less you see. We drag our blind, involuntary selves out of bed and present the body as a done deal. It is not. We are human. If you want no mistakes replace us with computers. Good luck with that. Thanks again. Is there someone else in the office I could speak to? The water is rising. I arrive in a place that looks nothing like Naples at 3.30pm thusly told the university I seek is in another country, at which point, none of that matters anymore, because they have stopped 'doing education', only reasonable coffee. The six minute commute takes forty-five with my face in the full gasmask of someone else's armpit. But nonetheless I arrive. Work.

Passive aggressive symbolic forms of violence are among the worst here, yes father-manager, you don't hit me, but you get away with talking violently outside the open office door when I am trying to work, a work you refuse to see as work, but play - being a product of a hammerheaded working class, like me - and doing that passive aggressive complaining and moaning behind my back, and sulking, and all that.

It would not only be easier but more productive and humane to hit me full in the face. Scream at me, tell me you don't want me here. You are a product of your own father's violence, but that violence is not stopped, it has morphed into more insidious - because less easy to counter - forms of oppression. Sharper elbows as stabbing points here. There are people wandering around who should know better who reckon that 'professionalism' is a stable paradigm. A neutral, grey concrete floor to be stood on. Look down, see twenty five stories of empty space, reel and feel the vertigo. Pathos. And here comes the whinnying voice again with the elbow blades scything 'don't pathologise'. What they are really saying is 'only we can do that.'

- exercise 4 -

Line all of the chairs up against one wall. Line all of the topless females against the other wall. Switch on both radios. Switch on the black slab. Stand on the table and make the following speech:

'I have been in the house of the dead with grandma and no shoes would fit her. I put the tiny shoe on my foot and she hammered a nail into it, and water poured out.' Get thee down from the table, go into the kitchen and collect all the buckets and basins thaa can find to catch the pouring water.

Act 32: On preferring the American remake

Coz it's funny.

Sick of people bleating on about how the original Girl With the Dragon Tattoo or whatever was a masterpiece whereas the US remake is a complete travesty coz it's merely not true.

Not that I particularly care, I mean, it merely gets on

my nerves. As does everything Jjjjzjzjz says actually.

The issue of the so-called inferior remake perhaps complicated by Michael Haneke's US remake of his own Funny Games. A shot-by-shot remake though, nevertheless, I maintain that each remains its own separate and distinct film: a film about northern European violence is one thing; a film about American violence something altogether different. The meaning of the violence changed.

Take the end of Funny Games (either version), and take this digression for what it is: a digression... what if the wife had never been walked to the yacht thus eventually pushed into the lake; what, instead, if she'd been left, alone, in the summer-house, on a chair, and what if the torturers had merely decided that enough was enough and disappeared, never to return, and the wife was left sat alone on a chair wondering what came next.

Plus, as well, the number of people I have killed for

saying the book's so much better than the film, when
– clearly – a book could never be better than a film
stands at, as of today, 39.

Act 33:

Later: the underground market collapses through the
ceiling of your memory and suddenly it's 1992 and
you're stood in a toilet cubicle with your mate, the
pair of you passing back and forth a bottle of amyl
nitrate, getting the stall-holder to doctor a receipt so
you can skim two quid back from your employers.
Suddenly the undergraduate marking symbolises
another privileged life altogether and absolutely fuck
all, exactly simultaneously.

Act 34 AKA 42 vi:

'The problem of beginnings, of rousing sufficient
energy to try again after the failure of the last time
and the memory of the failures preceding those. If

you want to write just do so: open up a word.doc and hit the keys without looking where your fingers are landing, anything just to make marks on the whiteness; the corruption of it all. Some of my best poems were written that way, even though I don't write poems or have ever aspired to write them. An overused, stupid, debased word. The bible is full of them – which I write without any understanding at all of what I might be trying to get at. Enacting my own advice as I wonder if I can really be arsed giving it one more try.

I am confident that I am a nice guy; confident that anyone – willing to make the effort – could get to like me; it's just that… all that business of letting people know you're actually open to them getting to know you; that you would positively like them to get to know you. All the signs and indications necessary to convey this. The complexity of the discourse. How time consuming it is. I am a nice guy so please make the effort to see through my externals and get to like me.

Clothes as well, I mean; clothes. I suppose all this - sweeps hands down over body and outwards - will require changing. This t-shirt I have had nearly 15 years, bought from the Tib Street Army Surplus store; a few – several – holes of varying sizes beneath the arm but, so what, when do I ever raise my arm, either to volunteer for something or to request to speak. A perfectly fine shirt. And this, this… that my father spent the last year of his life in: a touch big but, again, so what; perfectly serviceable. Though I suppose 'the woman' will disagree. As well, my weight… don't eat this, don't eat that, I expect. I've had 6 sugars in my coffee as long as I can remember but I imagine that'll cut no ice with her; I imagine the sugar will have to go. Or be reduced. Or exchanged for sweetener. Clothes and weight. The impact upon my wardrobe and larder 'the woman' will make…

Though perhaps I'm just looking for excuses; reasons for inaction. Can I really continue much longer like this. Wallowing in my own filth. Unlovely and unloved. Would buying a new t-shirt be so much of a sacrifice, really? I mean, really? The loss of a few pounds in exchange for a new garment, the necessary condition of the humanizing presence of another in my life.

How afraid I am of ending up one of those old guys in the pub, alone; the far end of the bar; staring into their pint and their outspread tabloid. Anything to avoid that conclusion to my life. Though, yes, undoubtedly I am 'stuck in my ways', somewhat.

And what of writing? The time lost at garden centres and furniture warehouses and suchlike... Traipsing around after her; holding her coat; having opinions about stuff. What do I know of plants and flowers and interior design? Well, the fact is I know lots about such matters but what time do I have to expound upon those subjects, as expound I will surely be expected to do? I'm better off on my own. Yes, I think I'm better off alone. Better off alone. I think I'm better off… Yet, for all that…

I must carry on. I can't carry on; I must carry on. Try again, fail again; fail better 'lol'. Which is a laugh. Carrying the weight of each past failure up and down the daily trudge of Chester Road, forever. One foot in front of the other for the rest of my life until I find myself walking backwards. Ridiculous to talk of a past, even; more accurate to think of my life story as birth – failure – now. Oh the infinite elasticity of my failure. My writing the only thing I have keeping me getting up in a morning. The putting of one word in front of the other until I find myself writing backwards. So of course I must carry on. The writing needs to happen. Writing as a threshing through the undergrowth and foliage of my life despair to try to arrive at some kind of clarity; as necessary to me as breathing.

Carrying on as *carryon*.

Though for all that how necessary is it really… Oh this endless swinging from pole-to-pole. I can't cope with it no longer.

I must write.

I must ease the pain of this isolation; bring back to life muscles which, by now, due to their prolonged inactivity, may have lost all memory of the uses they were originally created for.

I must, once again, move in time to the ancient rhythm of the swamps as all our forefathers and forebears did.

Such imperatives and yet – for all of that – I find myself prevented from acting; prevented by my own bad life choices and blind mistakes only. I need to clear my head. I need some fresh air'.

42 vii:

And so saying Mendellsohn rises, pulls closer the

lapels of his jacket, and heads towards his front door determinedly; behind which he expects to find – fully expects to find – a path down to the quiet road upon which he lives which, in its turn, will feed onto the main highway into the metropolis… where we find him now, having abandoned the seemingly fruitless wait for a bus, striding hurriedly and distractedly toward his destination: the city. There Mendellsohn goes: scowling at teens in groups; women pushing buggies; solitaries idling on corners… scowling at trees; houses; convenience stores and people with quite clearly visible disabilities…

- interlude (even meaner while) –

16m ago Egypt to extend state of emergency for 3 months

19m ago UK may use taxes to inhabit tech giants to do more to fight extremism, minister says

24m ago Iran's leader blames enemies for unrest as

death toll rises

30m ago Uganda's Museveni signs law removing age cap for president

35m ago Boeing talks not considering change of control at Embraer

36m ago New drug approvals hit 21-year high in 2017

37m ago Israel changes law to make it harder to cede Jerusalem control

38m ago North Korean Olympic overture seen aimed at blunting international pressure

40m ago Speculators raised net short bitcoin positions in Dec 26 week

42m ago LeEco founder defies China return order, stays in U.S. for car fundraising

44m ago BP takes $1.5 billion hit over U.S tax changes, joining Shell

45m ago European winners and losers after U.S. tax overhaul

54m ago U.S. airport immigration computers go

down temporarily

57m ago Speculators raised net short bitcoin positions in December 26 week

1h ago Airbus delivered over 700 jets in 2017, met tarinhabit

1h ago Ireland seeking to sell 3-4 billion euros of 10-year debt

1h ago Two shells from Syria hit southeastern Turkey

1h ago South Korea offers talks with North ahead of Olympics

1h ago Australian investigators to raise seaplane in which Compass Group CEO, family killed

1h ago Bankers to burn midnight oil ahead of 'MiFID' dawn

Black Keys

Pia pia piano, piano, piano pia pia piano, piano, piano

Act 35: Colour Plates

Steps up to railway station between a railway arch and a pub; sooty, blackened brickwork; sandblasting required. Cigarette advertising and a make of beer which no longer exists. No people.

A stretch of grass; a small plane and numerous people in a row looking out from the observation deck.

Foreground of people. On-going construction to the right; above the road can be seen semi-finished aerial walkways intended to eventually connect building to building. Records for sale.

Aerial walkways branching off from a central tower; all concrete. Domestic residences. Concrete bollards. Children at play. An old lady walks away in the opposite direction holding a child by the hand.

Concrete flyover. City-scape in distance. Minimal traffic.

Footbridges disappearing into the distance at regularly placed intervals over a wide dual carriageway; the lanes of the carriageway are separated by snooker table smooth areas of grass.

Gents boutique, owned by a footballer; a barber's next door.

Excessive reliance on the colour red in the construction of the outfit. Spectators appear 'nonplussed'.

Directions to car and coach parks. A clock. No notion, presently, of all the future incarnations of the building. The time is half past six. Or was half past six. Or will be half past six in approximately six hours and 40 minutes.

A statue on a plinth between a camera shop and a black cab. Who is the statue of? What did they achieve to merit the building of such a statue? Passers-by in the foreground consider or are oblivious to the future direction of the art of statuary. On the horizon looms a crane.

WILLIS FITTED FURNITURE CENTRE.

White buildings blackened with soot and the everyday

grime of the city. Palace of a newspaper magnate and a bank. A lady in tan stockings pauses on her way to check the heel of her shoe.

'Studio'; an orange and white double-decker bus; a white tower with a point; a dark red, brownish tower – nearer – emblazoned with the word 'refuge'; a white building, soot blackened; the number '206'.

Disappearance of an entire street. 'Now Leasing'. Disappearance of grass and trees.

'No parking' disregarded. Parking occurring. A corrugated iron roof at an acute angle. A foreground prime for redevelopment.

The landlord and landlady's head just visible over the bar. The joy or proprietorship. Two unoccupied stools. Two patches cleared in a dusty window.

M Symphony Orches

Tatler. 'who did cock robin?' To become the site of countless hundreds of lost but not wasted hours. The lady in the heavy green coat with her arm outstretched, the hand holding an envelope, about to post her letter.

Bright lights; short skirts and *Shaft's Big Score*.

Alvin Stardust's head painted on the side of a house. A mural for all seasons.

Excessive reliance on the colour pale green in the construction of the outfit. Spectators appear 'preoccupied'.

White Keys

Pia pia piano, piano, piano pia pia piano, piano, piano pia pia piano, piano, pi

Act 36: Unfilmed Michael Haneke script #2

A successful businessman, well respected in society, holding down a good job with a nice home and a wife and two kids, is at the heart of an online ring circulating documents and paraphernalia relating to the deaths of celebrities. This includes close-circuit videos from the homes of celebrities, sometimes capturing the deaths of the celebrities on tape; autopsy films and documents; and assorted medical records.

Long, static shots of the man, alone, late at night, in a dark room, intently watching the images of dying celebrities on his computer.

Something happens, then something else happens then a final thing happens.

Act 37:

Field Day festival Day 2, Victoria Park, London, some point in the past.

Here to see The Fall; to show The Fall to the person I'm with.

Numerous rows culminating in, eventually, a relationship ending (a decision not taken by me) just a couple of days after that performance by the group. Wondering as to the possible role of The Fall in the ending of that relationship.

The process by which real-life pain is transformed into a semi-amusing anecdote.

However, many years later stood with Sal in front of the stage at Victoria Warehouse in Trafford Park, the Fall just about to come on. A brilliant set. Strong and tight. Noticing the huge lump on Mark's forehead. Later, the fears for his health on the online forum followed by, over the coming months, a series of cancelled dates and performances.

Mark's health really mattering to me though I've never met him or spoke to him or anything like that; have only seen him and group a countless number of times; the first time some 25 years ago at The Roadhouse.

Act 38:

Fucking hell Richard is there any point carrying on? Look at that fucking photo of fucking Kim Jong Un with the penis microphones and the big gold plastic cock between the hammer and sickle. Look at Trump's flabby rotten peach of a head with tiny ceramic dentures inserted, their vicious hardness in diametric opposition to his sick marshmallow oompa loompa bonce. They would cut right through your flesh and bone and from there you would merely be assimilated into the orange wife flesh. Jeff Nuttall was right. There are some who have known nothing but a world that could be wiped away in minutes and a few now - only a tiny handful left - who remember it as permanent. No wonder it's nuts out there. No wonder nobody gives a shit. I'd stop writing and go have a wank but the Sertraline renders the attempt futile. No wonder everyone is just out for themselves. This is the No Future Rotten was on about.

This crisis calls for a more international kind of swearing. France. Le coo-yon de chien - the dog's bollocks. Norway. Yan-te-loven - Folk that reckon they're better than others (pejorative). Maybe we should be kinder, to Fukuyama.

The fucking hippies reckon they get it. They buy Ecover shit then drive to France. Green petrol stations down the Calder Valley and the point where there is a direct correlation between their business and that station's daily activities and its consequences: the flood; pictures of flooded petrol stations in the Calder Valley, next to the litany of pictures of lifeboat parades in the late nineteenth and early twentieth century. This is what premonitions are, not real messages from the future but messages from the past that happen to act as such by sheer accident.

But still these tree-hugging pothead imbeciles spout their sanctimonious moron music. No wonder half the products they get sold are about having a cleaner shit. Ecover, Ecover, Ecover, the mantra as the worry beads are passed through the hands, but it all goes down the drain. This is the problem when psychoanalysis has been thrown out. They all need fucking psychoanalysts. Those folk. You know the ones. Preserving indigenous vegetables to add to snake venom, frotting caterpillars, living in a tree. All in the name of your God Sustainability except all you do brings Her less into focus, makes her fade like some poor soul caught in a fucked transporter on a 1970s episode of Star Trek. I am not a climate change denier, it is happening now. None of us are sustainable, there is only vital, necessary. The future is a future where everyone is unsustainable, but some are much less sustainable than others. These treehouse dwellers are only ushering that future in as much as if they are waving the gas vans through the gate into the field in a traffic warden's uniform. The cloth sack that used to be filled with polystyrene beads. Trolley bags heavy as corpses, the size of corpses, legs tucked under chin before rigour mortis sets in, asked to sit there, like that, then blam, zip, wheel...

Act 39:

Soylent Green Weather. Sweaty and cold at the same time, a real-time crisis unfolds. Someone on The Circuit calls it 'Harsh Mild'. The averaging of all weathers into Harsh Mild, unweather, exposure to which brings pneumonia-like symptoms and inevitable death. Po-mo cool, austerity hot.

Schools are ghettoes for young humans, one of the most disempowered groups in society. Gated communities are ghettoes of fear and pernicious class and status anxiety. These symptoms should be pathologised as much as those of people awarded ASBOs. Walk around and ask why zebra crossings? Why bus stops? Why pavements? Why shoes? I get shoes. But what about the rest of it? Is it all still vitally relevant? Just after you've been born the year you were born in was the only one (Heidegger) but then people from 1984 etc who don't remember the Berlin wall coming down show up. And then you start to reckon all over again: Perhaps this is the only personal benefit of teaching, beyond the cash, nous.

Act 40:

The stench as natural as a plastic bag. The facade one has to make of oneself every day in order to keep renewing oneself precisely in the form of that facade. Therefore one fears frankness. Austerity as a contradictory concept. But yet don't. Kirsty Allsop and make do and mend and the ludicrous hangover from the fuedal ancien regime. Pterodactyl.

You have become the totem, the kicky doll... It is time to get the spaces well away from here. A hundred miles then back to Manchester, paid later... no whiff, you are free, so be free, to pull out your money, go where you need, but also to commit to no more orders, as Graves said, as long as I live...

If you don' buy it and you don't. So get out be out be in the media be outspoken drop any pretence of worry about it, what comes comes. Staithes retreats loosen it... you die when you die...

Act 41:

The text is sick, subject to waking hallucinations and night-time bad-dreams. The cold sweat of disturbed sleep as the unconscious language cracks and begins to break apart losing the little coherence there at the beginning, appearing more disordered and jumbled. The text roams the streets of Frankfurt, naked, 1399, pursued to the ship of fools by mercenary seamen, their fists bulging with gold, expulsion from the city of literary fiction and Waterstones good-taste now an unavoidable reality, coming, at the end of the century to replace death in the anxious imaginations of western Europa.

'Things themselves become so burdened with attributes, signs, allusions that they finally lose their own form. Meaning is no longer read in an immediate perception, the figure no longer speaks for itself…'

- Foucault, Madness and Civilization

- interlude –

9m ago Trump targets book, threatens ex-ally Bannon with legal action

12m ago Sears Holdings to close 103 Kmart and Sears stores

15m ago U.S. suspending more than $255 million in security aid to Pakistan

26m ago Russia - U.S. call for U.N. emergency session on Iran is 'destructive'

26m ago Iranian army commander offers to help police suppress unrest

1h ago Trump to host bipartisan meeting on 'Dreamers' next week

1h ago Blast hits police in Afghan capital Kabul, dozens of casualties

1h ago U.S.-South Korea military exercises to start after Paralympics

1h ago Trump credits his firmness for potential Korea talks, signals Olympic concession

1h ago U.S. sanctions five entities tied to Iran's missiles programme

1h ago 2017 was second hottest year on record, after sizzling 2016

Act 42:

'Richard', my character: my underwritten, only semi-convincing character. What's his body shape and what does his face look like? What clothes does he wear? What does he sound like when he speaks? I have no idea. What is it that's caused me to so suddenly wonder about these questions? I look around to see if I can notice what the spur might have been . . . The words from the other room that might or might not be his . . . so faint that I can't quite pick them out. Am I overhearing a conversation or am I being addressed. Indistinct words. And yes I know my hearing is not all it should be for someone of my age but I feel surprised about having quite this much trouble hearing what's being said so nearby, it seems. The voice becoming slightly clearer as I take a couple of steps towards the back room where it now seems to be coming from. Remembering the sounds of the many different voices of some of the many people I've known throughout my life… Babble of intrusive chatter rising; from the back room that I'll be entering in a couple more steps which I realised, recently, after however long not spent noticing, needs redecorating badly; we need to redecorate that room I said to no one as there was no one but me present; we can't be having friends round with that room looking as that. Wondering about the rooms and the chairs of my other character, the more somewhat successfully sketched 'Steven' and 'Natalie'.

Right foot permanently hung, suspended, forever, on the verge of taking the step that I'm about to take but never quite manage to ----

Bergman's *Persona* and the numerous, lesser films influenced by it.

Is there a Steven and a Richard or is there, really, only one person who is me. Deep forensic work analysing the only evidence available: the text. Magnifying glasses and dusting for finger-prints...

And voices. Voices. Voices. Richard's voice and then Steven's drowning out Richard's voice being talked over by Richard who wonders about the eventual destination of the text – accompanied by the distorted musings of George Michael – which means the place where the text is taking him, or taking them, as long as they are able to maintain their mediumistic function of channeling the voices of this moment of right now-ness which their individual histories comprising, ever so miniscule threads in the history of forever, have led up to. M-m-mumming-uh…

Challenging the portrayal of voice hearing in popular culture… bearded loners hearing whispers instructing them to kill all the lovers they never had and such as… which we all know is bullshit; shameful, sensationalist and cheap bullshit… I write, wondering how your answering voice, Steven, is going to respond. Your voice that might be my voice or mine that might be yours.

A call; a response.

Not George Michael today but the voice of Chrissie Hynde circulating around and around in my head. You've changed. It was the talk of the town. Maybe tomorrow; maybe today… Another 80s singer. Another member of that brigade that meant something once but are now largely forgotten or, if not forgotten, remembered only by a handful of die-hard fans that, the older I get, seem to mean only the more to me, in contrast to years ago when those same people meant absolutely fuck all as far as I was concerned.

- interlude –

52m ago John Young, 'most experienced' U.S. astronaut, dies at 87

1h ago Japan's Abe urges central bank's Kuroda to keep up efforts on economy

1h ago VW 2017 group sales rose to around 10.7 million cars, beating Toyota

2h ago Cameroon separatist leader taken into custody in Nigeria

2h ago New Zealand's former deputy PM Jim Anderton dies, aged 79

2h ago France plans privatisation law in asset sale push

3h ago Eleven Saudi princes detained following protest over utility bills

3h ago Cornered Merkel launches talks with SPD in bid to secure fourth term

4h ago Trump rejects author's accusations, calls self 'stable genius'

4h ago Trump book author says his revelations will bring down U.S. president

4h ago Egypt's Coptic Christians celebrate Christmas amid tight security

4h ago May to rejig cabinet on Monday, senior ministers safe

4h ago Brutal cold snap stuns U.S. East Coast after blizzard

5h ago Williams paints benign picture of Fed rate hikes, strong U.S. economy

5h ago Peru's Fujimori calls for unity after controversial pardon

5h ago Thousands of Belgians brave cold to take dip in wintery North Sea

5h ago Caracas shops mobbed as Venezuela's Maduro

forces price cuts

5h ago Over 20 hurt as magnitude 5.1 quake jolts western Iran

5h ago Iran stages pro-government rallies, derides Trump 'blunder' at U.N

5h ago Arab League to lobby U.N. to recognise Palestinian state

Act 43:

The answer is boring because banal. Our chairs are just as fucked and unfashionable as anyone else's. Most of them came out of skips. The best stuff. The really shameful stuff I tried to make.

Act 44:

The fire in the block of flats, six months on from the Arena bomb, the *Manchester Evening News*, when one manages to crawl through the exowindows of Circuit advertising and feedback demands, reports with chest-beating pride that:

'People are handing coffee to the emergency services at the scene and offering people places to shelter. Manchester responding as Manchester always does.'

Apart, of course, from those times when 'Manchester' responds by screaming at homeless people for sitting near cashpoints or tells them to 'get a fucking job', or fucks someone over, roughly as described by a Shaun Ryder lyric, 1988-1991: To designate any object above a certain scale good or bad is as pointing to the moon and saying 'I only like the half that's always bright.'

Act 45:

The line between working and not-working has gone, but the DWP still enforce it. A Jobs Fair is held. The employers tell their own story. Army recruitment, adult social care and retail. I hear a member of staff saying 'get your sleeves rolled up, get your 'ands dirty', encouraging a claimant to go to the Wetherspoons stand. To try out for a chance to serve me, five years ago, when I would conclude each weekend in the converted cinema Wetherspoons at the end of Deansgate, a booth at the back, my paper spread out on the table before me, whatever book I was reading at the time on the seat beside me, finding it no effort whatsoever to block out the sound of the surrounding ambient chatter and focus on the words in front of me, focus on them as long as I could until the Stella made them blurry and start to move. Each Sunday night the same forever, until forever ended.

Universal Credit is new HISTORY.

Act 46:

My sister said she was going to come round to collect the Christmas tree. Then she said she wasn't as burning them does something to the chimney. So I said I'd sort it out. And on Friday night I set about the tree with an old saw of my dad's from the toolbox of his that still sits in the hall as I haven't thought of anywhere else to put it yet.

I sawed the top off. Then I sawed some branches off. Then I sawed another length off the trunk. Then the rest of the branches. What was left was a bit of a stump in the pot. Plus a load of branches all over the carpet.

I'll get the stump and roots out of the pot I said. I felt proper into doing it. So I had a go.

Eventually, it got sorted. Soil ended up everywhere, all over the carpet, all over the throw on the chair, all over my trousers, but, yes, it got sorted.

And then the bits of tree were bagged up and disposed of the following day.

And on my way out, later, I passed a Christmas tree, still in its full state, dumped on the pavement, dead, dry and brown. It was brittle and beginning to roll…

Act 47:

Little signals. 'Here is a towel for you' actually means the rest of us are about to eat and we have called twice can you stop writing and come out to join us now please? The repressed sign is not repressive, nor is the repression of the full demand to come in and eat uncivilised, in the everyday sense of that term.

- interlude -

58m ago No Grand Coalition! Opponents of Merkel alliance hit the road

1h ago Rohingya insurgents say 10 found in Myanmar grave "innocent civilians"

2h ago U.S. ultimatum on nuclear deal, new sanctions draw Iran threat

2h ago China says Iran nuclear deal not derailed, pledges constructive role

Act 48:

Overheard: 'My eyes are open now. Well, more than they were before. And I know that's not sayin' much, right...' Looking at houses in an estate agent window, 'dreams are sick'.

Act 49:

The humanities should be metaphysical, what use pushing them through the mincer of methods and ethics? The total living, walking contradiction reduced to horrible lines of fat blood and gristle? Writers, researchers and academics should be 'producing', rather than just reckoning, and producing outside of the seething paranoia of peer review, as well as putting risky things into those peer review bully circuits. We should be 'making' - as in poesis - and making speculative, risky, untested proposals: the humanities is not like physics. This should happen outside of the blind romance of party loyalty, or any philosophical doxa, but with an ever closer relation to the bleakest depths of our times.

We should be actively seeking to discover where we are wrong, not where we have got it right. Le Crayola Rouge.

Act 50:

Why can't I be a boy, the girl wonders; get to do exactly what I want and worry about pleasing no one but myself. Men have it so much better. They can sleep with whoever they want, whenever they want and no one judges them. I want that same freedom to do what I want whatever anyone else thinks. Girls are so judgemental. Boys seem to get along with each other easier; the obsession with appearing cool and not wanting to seem to care too much even when they spend every Saturday night alone at home drinking lager from the off-licence, crying and then thinking about phoning the suicide hotline.

I want to have sex whenever I want but I can't because of the fear of what my friends will think and because no one wants to have sex with me.

The Houellebecq thesis concerning the fates of those over-looked by the sexual revolution which never happened in this house anyway, this house that I will someday leave to go and live in a second floor flat with the person I plan to spend the rest of my life with, a future seeming very far-off and impossible from this point, busy shopping for futons in the futon place.

Walking up and down the aisle of stacked futons in the futon display room even though I am not entirely sure what a futon is; listening to the piped-music enter my ears and bounce off the bouncy surfaces of the futons onto the even bouncier surface of more expensively priced futons, that I hurry by looking for the futons that are more standardly priced, adroitly avoiding as I do, a couple of wealthy looking potential futon buyers who serve no purpose, the girl feels, other than to remind her of her none-couple status. I know what I like though and I like what I know the girl thinks, unless I'm wrong of course, and what I say I like is, really, just what my friends like which I've somehow convinced myself is what I like. I like my friends; like imagining the friends I'll one day have who, generally, all seem to bear strong resemblances to historical personages from the worlds of music, cinema and/or literature, or else, are all pretty identical reproductions of myself. Friends guide the culture. Friends guide my taste to the point where I no longer even know what I mean when I speak of 'my taste'. Though perhaps this is just how taste works: you start off with something which is indisputably your own and then over the years, depending upon the extent of your exposure to various whatnots and doobries, that thing you thought you once recognised and understood morphs into some huge, out-of-control beast with a mind and life of its own which, occasionally, every now and again, when you come face-to-face with it, causes you a moment of confusion and incomprehension as you realise it is something you think you should recognize but now no longer do. I like the bad-boys as I, myself, am a bad-boy trapped in a girl's body, the girl thinks; thinking, again, of the guy she has her mind set on that evening. The guy who, yes, though she knows he's worked his way round several of her friends, she doesn't care, who she's going to have and to have forever. Because that is important. Forever is key, thinks the bad-boy. The alpha-male, hunter-gatherer, leader-not-follower who knows who he has his eye on for that weekend and who the very lucky lady is who he'll be leaving he club with.

Death to couples!

Blood, brains, flesh, cartilage, bone, muscle, hair

flying left and right and centre, left and right and centre, right and left and centre… splattering all over the futons. Ruining them.

Here. Here is where we start to get to it. Where we start to hit on things in the spirit of what we set out to do.

But the point of the whole work is that you can't do it without going through the rehearsed words to find the slip, without sinking into the digressions and botched lines, without the banalities and outbursts, without the symptoms that are knots so tight they will never be untied… you have to try to bring out the repressed fantasies, the violent and unacceptable… Even if it means doing so in the names of others, ridiculous names, Gobert Raves even.

Here. Here is where we start to get to it. But of course then it slithers straight out of you fingers as though it had never manifested… this is the nature of the task at hand…

Act 51: (alternate version)

Who sleeps like that, wonders the girl, watching the pop video in her second floor flat; that artful arrangement of limbs; the angles and planes of that woman's body. A geometrical problem, beautifully lit, presented in a pop video; a geometrical problem or a geometrical solution. Unaware of the singer's gaze, as well. I can feel his eyes on me immediately when he looks over after entering the bedroom. Such bullshit, lying there like that pretending to have no awareness of his presence.

Act 52:

Memories. Heaton Moor. Everything is suddenly in bloom. Apparently Mani from The Stone Roses lives a few doors down. Maybe I'll knock on and tell him what I reckon of the new single. Perhaps not. We suspect we have had things from his skip now. Living the dream, or, er, dreaming about living. In the summer here the sound of lawnmowers, leaf blowers etc, who says there's no such thing as mass behaviour?

Idea: (abandoned, pretty much):

'The girls' (Claudia; Fatima; Gail et al) marauding through the city, Michelle as their leader, striking fear and terror into the hearts of all who they encounter; carrying out robberies and random, indiscriminate acts of violence etc. A kind of Kathy Acker-esque girl gang bringing to the text the necessary suspenseful highs and lows to ensure underground success and endorsement, thirty years in the future, when the authors are either past caring or dead, from some contemporary art-star or other. An idea abandoned due to fear of the research required likely resulting in the imprisonment of one of both of the authors, plus what's with the reliance on 50-odd year old plot devices? Oh why does the last thing I read succeed, every time, in erasing everything I read before?

Idea: (also abandoned, pretty certainly):

Some kind of secret society who believe that by their rites and rituals they're responsible for maintaining the balance and harmony of the world. They meet on the river bank at midnight to practice their dark arts. Kind of a Jacques Rivette, Out 1 'the 13' set-up; kind of Twin Peaks-y as well. Conflict between the girl-gang and the secret society? Conflict and tension prior to some sort of eventual resolution and transcendence? The importance of transcendence? How important is transcendence? An idea abandoned due to the difficulty of slotting this element into the already existing narrative fraguments; plus, as well, due to the fear of messing with forces that are not 'of this world'.

Actually what's much more scary is that there is no plot at all. Secret forces, of this world or not, are really fucking comforting, even Ernst Stavro Blofeld has men in bright overalls organising things into something like order. Even if it is in a hollow mountain full of nukes.

The real world now consists of hundreds of hollow mountains full of nukes not under any one ruling logos. Unlike Blofeld's order, the destabilised drives teem, they do not team...

I can hear the critics teeming in too, right at this point, 'fascist apologist!' They too, are part of the chaos and no, I am not for totalitarianisms... In they come, to make cunty ego-capital, tearing a bit off your calf with a butcher's knife and holding it aloft, bloody...

Idea: (saving it for the sequel)

It's Mendelsohn that Orlando meets outside Superdrug. Before arriving Mendelsohn sends Orlando a text saying he'll be the one carrying the big bunch of flowers, which is a joke that Mendelsohn is making, though a joke which Orlando doesn't immediately take as such. So in that instance what, exactly, is it that has happened to the joke? Who the hell knows. Though later, in the pub, where the pair of them will sit Orlando shall say to Mendelsohn 'would you like to see my ipod; have you ever seen an ipod before?' before proceeding to show the machine to Mendelsohn, including all of the many hundreds of songs for every occasion, even occasions such as the one the pair then find themselves in, that are stored on the ipod. The future will happen for Mendelsohn and Orlando, and it will happen in exactly the way that it should: couches will be slept on and chairs sat in and many, many films will be watched.

Act 53:

The Fall at Glastonbury. Seemed utterly pissed off with being there and each other. Heard they came in a helicopter to bypass everything that it was, that Glastonbury is. They played it out, hard and tight. It was saying 'all that shit out there is really sloppy'. In my head the helicopter is black. It might have been silver. Orange even. I never saw it. In my head it is black. I bought '45 84 89, the B Sides' in W.H. Smiths. It was the only Fall record there. It has that track that just goes 'win Fall CD' over and over on it, which is a piece of sheer genius. I was faced with that moment, that this is either one of the worst or one of the best things I have ever heard moment.

There is a link right back to my childhood in W.H. Smiths, Rochdale. I used to buy sci-fi with my pocket money there. 2000AD and then novels. I bought a Michael Moorcock book called *The Rituals of Infinity*, which I thought was brilliant. Then I bought some Elric book and horrified, left it alone for a while. Then I got a Jerry Cornelius book. I still have all the good ones and from the publishing dates I can see that I was probably 14 years old. So at that age I got Miss Brunner and Catherine Cornelius and Bishop Beasley, Mo Collier, Jerry with his dick out, all processed through Ballard and Burroughs.

So then years and years later and I'm talking to Michael Butterworth...

Act 54:

Zizek said blood brings change. Hegelians do it with longer curves, and with Zizek there is comedy. Gillian Rose said the Broken Middle means that the speculative standpoint is lost, the place you used to stand in, in all the daily addictions you pay for, but... the middle being broken means it is open, not morbidly closed. If she were alive she would probably say this means more than coping, it means shaping. So you go beyond 'Donald' and go straight to utopian reckoning. But utopian reckoning as negation: Saying no until you reach the yes. Joseph Campbell said a country that no longer believes in its own myth cannot exist. It feels like that. Mmm but America is a prism and each facet holds a different mytheme and they overlap... through the prism...

In California it has been raining since September, this rightward shift is a clampdown in light of Knowledge with a Capitol K.

- "Basically, it's all about the micro bu-bubbles" (after Michel de Certeau) -

09:43: Begin writing postcards I bought from the gift-shop.

09:49: consider various Vatican intrigues involving the sale of shoddy goods out of gift shops.

09:53: a Demdike Stare CD.

09:54: reply to Circuit messages from S-.

10:14: a handful of new pens.

10:18: Remember imminent hospital appointment with orthopaedic consultant.

10:23: Try each of my new pens to make sure they're working by scribbling on a piece of scrap paper. After satisfying myself that each pen is indeed working I then tear the piece of paper up.

10:37: think about getting a glass of water.

10:41 email. Extract: "Currently Foucault is debating with some Maoists the best form of people's justice in a revolutionary situation. The Maoists support peoples courts; Foucault opposes peoples courts as he reckons they always get taken over by the bourgeoisie".

11:29 'I could explain what to do…'

11:35 think about going to the toilet.

11:41 go to the toilet.

12:44 Tesco.

12:44 Alternatively, Booths.

12:45 "it sells stuff that I know I like eating and, plus, I know where everything is in there. Don't wanna go somewhere new and have to start messing about".

13:42 J- walks past and I think about catching his eye in order to start a conversation. I decide not to though.

14:39 'The Kaiser Chiefs'.

14:45 various retail outlets in Leeds.

14:50 the smell of hand-sanitizer.

14:53 Wonder at not having missed my green jumper. Put it in my bag.

15:45 think about getting a coffee.

16:17 email. Unabridged: "H- did summat bizarre before, blew his nose into his hanky then tried going up to the women showing them his hanky".

16:42 reply to Circuit messages from S-.

17:07 think about leaving. Think about going for a glass of water and a break. *17:11* decide to go get a glass of water and to have a break.

17:33 consider the various positions of Foucault and his interviewers with regard to the judicial system; popular justice and contradictions within the working class.

17:35 think about leaving.

17:35 decide I will leave in ten minutes.

17:36 go for a piss

17:43 begin packing my stuff up.

I am a girl and a gun… I am all that's ever needed. I am entering now. A girl and a gun. A blonde girl entering the home where the residing elder female is absent. Searching for clues to piece together the backstory behind the shadowy, elite organisation referred to as "the 13". Big data. The dark web. I never leave my home without a weapon. When walking down the street I occupy, always, only the central ground. On alert for assailants in bushes. It is possible to do a lot of damage with a correctly wielded front door key. There are only seven possible plots in the world and I am three of them, the graffiti said. These figures don't match up. The calculator is not helping. Fearing for his wife and child due to his gambling debts. Oh Dougie. Mobile-Disco Dougie who my dad laughed at, echoing across the years the sound of a dead dad's laughter at insurance scams involving kayaks and exotic foreign rivers (he's sorry but he doesn't remember the details). The residing elder female has been travelling, by some account, twenty-odd hours and more though the figures are uncertain. The mob. The dark web. How some men spend half their lives searching for substitute mothers and consequently the remaining half, once they've found someone to occupy that role, resenting the person so behaving. Sadly, there is no fourth alternative.

To surrealism's skull piles signifying something urgent and important about death.

Black Keys

Ulrich! Ulrich! Ulrich!

Act 55:

'They are playing at playing a game. They are playing at not playing a game. If I show them I see they are, I shall break the rules and they will punish me. I must pay their game, of not seeing I see the game...'

- R.D. Laing, Knots

She feels like she's in some modernist poem; avant-garde stylings; fragmentation. The creation of some first year creative writing student who has read a couple of anthologies but not much else. The creative writing students sit around in the break-out area before the reading, lounging on brightly coloured, low-backed chairs, and they chat about their latest projects. What are you working on? What are you working on? I'm working on ---------; I'm working on ------------.

She understands that there's next to no difference between being the product of a current students mind and being the product of a former students, just time. They know about the seven possible plots. They know about Propp. I try so hard to avoid the cliché of being an ex student who moans on and on about current students. So boring; so predictable. From nowhere, two strangers appear: a man and a woman. No one recognises them; they are not from here; neither of them are on this course in this university. The superstar of poetry is with them. The woman disappears; the man and the superstar sit down at a table together. I will go over and I will invite the superstar of poetry to sit at this table, with us, the most confident of the young creative writing students thinks; though I can see that man she's sat with, due to me not recognizing him, due to me never having seen him before anywhere within this university, I – yet – cannot see him. I just assume she is only sat with him, to be sat – also – with the woman when she returns from wherever she left for - presumably the toilet - out of politeness as she didn't want to join our table uninvited.

She feels like her head is splitting up into the fragments of the poem, like she once knew stuff but now knows absolutely nothing at all. She wonders what could have happened. Her life following the outline of every poem ever written containing an insufficiently drawn 'you'. The portrayal and development of her life in all the erratically published poems, online and on paper; all the 'you's' being her; all written by the young, virginal boy poets determinedly cultivating the image of the great lover. The romantic misadventure and devastation of all involved here, in this brightly furnished break-out area. It's not that I hate only students it's that I hate near enough everybody. So that saves me, right? You former creative writing student. Accusingly. Accusatorily. I hate myself as well, of course. I hate myself as well. I just want to learn something to teach others how to learn the same thing so that they, in their turn, can teach the same stuff to the next lot to sit outside the reading venue, slouched in the chairs, telling each other about what they're all working on.

STOP IT! she wants to scream from the safe isolation of her room; all those kids all so sure of the imprint they're going to leave on the culture; the few of them dreaming of effecting some great, permanent change to the state of things via their words. Stop it. Any day spent locked-up writing while your loved one is busy elsewhere is a day wasted; you should be with the person you love. Write, sure; whatever; do what you like – everyone's got something they're into, be it writing, cooking or doing the garden; but remember it's more important to be a man than it is an artist. A man. A woman. A person.

Focus on the reward of a life well lived now rather than hoping for great things in the future, because all the future will bring will be your death and then what will the tributes on the national news mean.

And the superstar of poetry proves herself, also, a superstar of etiquette and manners and, thereby, immeasurably cooler than the young creative writing student.

The thing that she knows, there, alone in her room, is that she, herself, is a poem, constructed from a line here, and a line there, in the poems of others – all men. Self-constructed, her own poem. The narrowing to nothingness of the gap between art and life. Her life the only work that matters; the act she has devoted more time to than any other.

What she doesn't know is that her continued absence from the office is being so closely monitored by the man who, everyday, walks past the place she used to sit, the place where she'll be sitting no longer; she doesn't know that that same man is going to make enquiries amongst her colleagues tomorrow to try to find out where she is and that, sometime the following week, her phone will go and it'll be him and he'll say some things and then ask her some other things, one of which will be the question 'what's happened?'. At this point in history, in this precise place, she knows none of this. Though knowing it wouldn't help as, when the question comes, she won't have the first idea of how to respond.

Act 56:

The myth of the dirt-poor academic: what we are actually doing is managing the fudged interplay between the state and the private sector; this is not our business. As the risk is piled on the consumer... are you risky?

No mortgage then, risk transferred from capital onto the individual.

Here is the mort in mortgage. The state was meant to shelter the individual to enable them. No more. No more. I work all the time but my paid work is only a tiny part of my work. The infrastructural situation is behind what I and we are doing. Everyone sees everyone else's issues, in open plan offices, it's a control mechanism encoded with the structural rhetoric of transparency. When jobs become work and work becomes life. I need to be more distant and even more of a dissident from the left to be a better leftwinger, Blanchot. I need to loosen my hold to tighten my grip. Foucault - another kind of ordering - the authority of the discourse is what must be crumbled.

Act 57:

What is the new discourse? Abbreviated language in the young, 'whatevs', coupled with intensities, 'really really', 'proper proper'. The brevity indicates dismissal, the elongation and repetition is an alert to the importance of what is being claimed in a world over-saturated with the noise at the edge of communication.

Act 58:

The internalising of nations is their internment. In the Netherlands the PM says those who don't respect customs should leave. Customs. Not only the folk ritual, but the savage border...

- interlude –

10m ago Egypt's Sisi to run for second term in March election

10m ago Ex-military chief of staff to run in Egyptian presidential election

10m ago Pope Francis in Peru urges society to combat 'scourge' of corruption

14m ago Trump decries 'permissive' U.S. abortion

laws at rally

18m ago With no deal in sight, U.S. Congress faces looming government shutdown

20m ago Trump administration says U.S. mistakenly backed China WTO accession in 2001

42m ago What happens in a U.S. government shutdown?

42m ago Twitter to notify users exposed to Russian propaganda during U.S. elections

1h ago U.S. approves possible sale of F-35 jets to Belgium for $6.5 bln

Act 59 i:

Her father telling her, when she was a girl, about how his parents having nothing pushed him to go out and get everything he ended-up with, he wanted something different for himself. Her own mother and father… her wanting for herself just exactly the same thing as they had; that relationship. That kind of love.

We want it for ourselves but to what extent is that wanting, also, a wanting to please our parents; to try to validate the choices they made by repeating those same choices ourselves. The girl wanted a relationship, desperately, but didn't know how to go about getting one. Past strategy had always been to sit back and let people come to her. And people came. People were drawn to her. Men at work; at uni… later, married men who'd read my poetry or been somewhere I was whilst I read my poetry out and who'd then got in touch, ostensibly, to discuss that poetry and their own and then things had developed from there. The lifetime of sitting back and letting things happen hadn't brought the girl much in the way of results she knew and so would wonder, from time to time, if different tactics might be called for. What is wrong with me? Why do I spend all my free time alone, either here, in this house, or out somewhere such as a library or cinema; a place where solitary people don't feel too conspicuous? By your age, now, you should have a family of your own; I should be going visiting you for Christmas, her father had said to her one year before instantly backtracking with apologies. The thing was though, the girl knew her dad was right yet she didn't know why things kept, repeatedly, not happening for her.

Act 59 ii:

In America the new president signed executive orders to ban funding for international groups that provide abortions, and placing a hiring freeze on non-military federal workers. Blaming the oil peak is pointless, the disasters will be natural, then war, then nuclear...

Dub 4:

The red drink separatist dub balance idiot. The up with it toos inhabit burbles, echoing. The kind who 'only goes to the White Hotel now', if scaled and pitiless, I sign off the caches: Fire when ready; they do sit ups as the extremists dance to the film on future fire.

Its jubilant flaming passes the 'whatevs' test. She bore out the hair-changed class amid the 1h chairs of my day.

The world jokes behind the controversial anonymous economy. Manchester always the 15m to the one second. A personal window unrest. The seeing-to. Fucked hardest at the bedside of root. Creation central are the hosts, those that can't are the sale that The Shin is working. The musical wife, following Chris, who hires what he can through adult mythemes x

- interlude –

14m ago Arab refugees march in German city hit by far-right protests

25m ago Libyan forces clash with Islamic State near Dhara oilfield

42m ago Pressure mounts on Poland to back away from Holocaust bill

1h ago With an eye on Russia, U.S. to increase nuclear capabilities

1h ago Explosive memo released as Trump escalates fight over Russia probe

2h ago Turk border guards shoot at fleeing Syrians

Act 60:

Pop star deaths rarely move me, nor do I ever feel attracted to them. Mark Fisher's death didn't really until I saw the photo of his little boy: Then sadness like the deeps. Just writing this it strikes me that Mendelssohn's bible book – in its first incarnation - was finished and delivered by the printer on Friday 13th, the day Mark Fisher took his own life. Fisher was instrumental to Zero Books and left with the other good people, Tariq Goddard for one, who set up Repeater, who initially took the book on... it came out of the desperate near to death ash of my own life in 2014, as much as the living-on-dust texts of those two thousand and more years ago...

- skit -

1981, heading home to the rent-controlled apartment we're sharing. The uncollected garbage has begun to smell unbearable in the heat; it's everywhere, I say 'garbage' now... Soylent Green ghosts everything now... The streets empty of people at this time of day, most of our neighbours I expect still not having risen following the revels of last night, not that last night was anything particularly special, it's just that the night-time is when we come to life, when we make our history. My Midwest hometown still present, somewhat, in my mind but feeling further away than ever today; this is a movie that we're making; my reinvention as a downtown art-star; the 80s have begun and with this decade will come fame, sex and glamorous death. I can't wait to get home to tell Richard about the new piece I started in the studio today; pushing open the door of our apartment, I call out 'Richard!' to be met with the response 'Steven!', to be met with the sight upon entering the living space of Richard tied to a chair, his glasses skewwhiff across his face… 'Richard', I say 'what happened?' 'We were robbed! They tied me to this chair!' ' What did they take?', I ask. 'They took everything!'

- paraphrase of scene featuring Jean-Michel Basquiat and Keith Haring from Downtown 81, screened as part of Basquiat, Boom for Real exhibition at the Barbican

Act 61:

Humanities and no political bias in universities. So it is all bonkers, maybe it should all go... But then I walk out and the underlit ghoulish face of George Galloway hangs over Desi Point and suddenly it looks like 'Dead Point'... Up and across town the day after, a very particular sort of graffiti art prepares the ground for the back streets to become front streets... as a ritual purification, then more news...

- interlude –

1h ago Turkish helicopter shot down by Kurdish militia in Syria's Afrin

1h ago Merkel dodges question on Poland's new Holocaust law

1h ago Amid Olympic thaw, Pence says allies united in isolating North Korea

1h ago Kim Jong Un invites South Korean president for summit

2h ago Putin urges Netanyahu to avoid escalation in Syria

3h ago U.S. 'strongly supports' Israel's right to defend itself

3h ago Trump says Democratic memo on Russia is

'very political,' needs redactions

4h ago Italians march against racism after shooting spree against migrants

5h ago North and South Korea celebrate peace through taekwondo

- exercise 5 –

I begin in my own library with a Penguin Thesaurus and a two volume Oxford English Dictionary, the Oxford Shorter. I also select the Eric Partidge abridged Dictionary of Historical Slang, you must never omit the counterlanguage, but you can go with an old fashioned archive of it, as I am here. Partridge was born 1894 and died 1979.

I begin by selecting two words. With two words rather than one there is a dialogue, immediately, if only an obscure one.

I want to ask whether to begin with Volume 1 of the Oxford Shorter (A-M)? I flip a ceramic Yes/No coin I picked up at the Stoke ceramics biennial in 2015. The result is 'No'. So I go to Volume 2 (N-Z0).

It has 2515 pages. A random number generator selects page 1986 from pages 1307-2515. 1986: I see a year date already, not just a random number, as my mind introjects my own history. You must not resist these processes, you must mine them, train yourself to become attuned to what is happening and use them.

Page 1986 has three columns, so back to the random generator to select a number from 1-3. The third column is chosen. This column has eight full entries, so I generate another random number.

Squab: Thick, clumsy form, of the body, short and stout, but also undeveloped young birds. It has the sense of clumsy. I repeat the process for second word. Appogiatura. A grace note, or passing tone, prefixed as a suport to an essential tone or melody in music. Squab. Appogiatura. Unmelodious and melodious appear in my head. Add them in. 'Unmelodious squab and melodious appogiatura.' This is fancy language.

It is as difficult to erase the traces as it is to find them. Now I have 'launched'. I keep going with this process until I feel I cannot go forward.

Act 62:

Radical Philosophy, 2013; *Thesis 11*, 2010, I was leaving that place; 2008, I was teaching there; 2003 I was doing my MA; 2001, blimey.

Dub 5:

The horror of Mendelssohn's helicopter combat control, a separatist entity. The eager feel of the 2008 semen role. Petrol for the geist position, harmony cusp stuff. The 'glory be out' instead o' the dark limit. Jazzman. Plays of roguery. IBM Fox Google America calls. My market dream calculation took you in. You qualify evermore for time meddles. Looked at one way a map is neither an indexical or iconic sign. It's all Pollock spatter.

Act 63:

1998 I was a graphic designer at the Halifax, reading Marcuse locked in a room waiting for stats for the Report and Accounts of an institution already contributing strongly to the coming collapse of 2008. 1995, after three years of hedonism reading the beats and avant-garde novels of my Eng Lit. housemates, hallucinating the faces of all those unknown women as the weather, filling the whole of the sky that I walked beneath, walking the crap streets of that crap town where I still am and that I still, nonetheless, love - though, Sal, I would've left a couple of years ago, honestly - the names, the names of those women... Tilda Swinton, future bit-part player of my then unwritten poetic grief epic, the genesis of which lay in my sudden late thirties orphanhood, all those references to 'you' in my lines; that great dispersed and varied 'you' meaning… who exactly? My suspicion of that 'you' as opposed to my easy acceptance of the more traditionally suspect 'I' of poetry… self-erasure. Always looking around at how everyone else is behaving trying to figure out how I, myself, should behave; past 40, even now… The pretence of that 'you'; the creation of a life-story across the irregularly and obscurely published poems that corresponded, hardly at all, to the reality of my life as I perceived it back then…

…when I just about graduated into nothing and decided to 'begin' study. I had no idea that Thesis Eleven and Radical Philosophy existed.

…The title of the paper I gave at Salford University's conference on The Fall which now escapes me; something to do with Mark Smith's auto-didacticism.

Act 64:

Like the hero of every hot young American film-maker's first film, wandering around the city doing, well, not very much at all: meeting strange and fascinating characters; having non-sequitur heavy conversations; waiting beside or in front of the city's landmarks… the girl, or the boy, depending on the state of the culture at that particular moment of history, the girl or the boy with their Wine, Cinema and Greek Islands cuts across Piccadilly Gardens, stepping over the tramlines, avoiding the early evening rush of people keen to get home, and fixes their eyes on the Superdrug shop-front, deciding where they're going to stand to await the arrival of the person they'll, shortly, be meeting for the first time after however many conversations on the phone. To what extent will the window display of various pharmacy whatnots and annual holiday necessities affect their decision? Will they choose to stand in such a way that the sign blaring out 'buy one, get one free' is obscured to passersby or else will they take-up such a position as to imply that they, themselves, are the special offer, the eager listener to the tales of the old-jazzman against the background of a poster for a semi-forgotten Nicholas Ray film? Next to no equipment and next to no interest in taking part in the venture beyond a wide pool of friends all eager to be involved however they can, the girl gang marauding through the city, striking terror into the hearts of all, ending-up, for now at least, abandoned... Will the impulse to lift the bag, momentarily left unattended on the pavement, be possible to resist or else will she/he be returning home with a haul of uncertain origins? A kids surprise of kittens and kittens and kittens remembering the remark of Sontag's, possibly (unless it was entirely invented) that every biography is, simultaneously, a biography of place; these first features evidencing the very real, unarguable truth of that as our girl takes us – our girl or our boy – past more Manchester sites: the fountain in Piccadilly gardens; the grey, fat slug of queen Victoria in the same place; the Arndale bus station; the escalator down to the underground market. Sites, some of which, exist now only in memory – hers, his or whoever. It doesn't matter.

- interlude –

6m ago Tory MP calls government Brexit advice to firms "extraordinary"

10m ago Maintaining customs union will sell UK's Brexit short, trade minister says

10m ago Putting pressure on May, Labour backs new customs union with EU

1h ago U.S. labour agency overturns major ruling, citing Trump appointee's conflict

1h ago Delta, United Airlines become latest companies to cut NRA ties

1h ago Georgia lawmaker threatens to kill Delta state tax breaks over NRA stance

1h ago Amid fresh Trump tension, negotiators seek progress on NAFTA

Act 65: Love and Happiness (reprise)

'She is devoured, by him being devoured by her devouring desire to be devoured He is devoured by her being devoured by him not devouring her...'

- R.D. Laing, Knots

Kev was looking again at Michelle's Circuit page. She says 'cinema' instead of 'movies'. This is important. Kev's local off-licence had started stocking red and black Oranjeboom at 8.5%. His fourth can was open, in his hand; drinking and looking at Michelle's photos. She says cinema rather than going to the movies. Where had she been today? Kev had walked past her desk three times over the course of the day and not once had he seen her.

His favourite photo of Michelle was the one of her in the chair, her expression seeming to, simultaneously, acknowledge and yet challenge the void that faces each and every one of us on this earth that threatens to, daily, subsume us all. Kev looked forward to the time when he could share with Michelle his own experience of the void, imagining the moment when the light of recognition would illuminate her whole person. Why had she overlooked him for so long, she'd wonder? What would come after that moment, though, Kev was less certain about. He wished he'd bought six cans from the shop instead of merely the four; trying to decide whether he could be bothered going back for another couple. He concluded that he could. What did he care what the woman in the shop thought of him. Of course he liked that photograph. She doesn't love me but that doesn't negate my love for her. My love is legitimate and can be considered real regardless of the fact that it isn't reciprocated. I like being in love, which I am, with her: she who no one's seen for days. Have the conversations we have had – the few words we've exchanged – left any imprint on her at all; does she ever think of me? Every night I can barely wait for the following day so I can be at work again; so I can walk by her desk; so I have the possibility of crossing paths with her to perhaps say something to her. It doesn't matter that she doesn't love me back. This is a special position I'm in; one known to everyone at one time or another in their life, I'm sure; unexamined, though – this unreciprocated love; and special for that reason.

In my delirium I feel like a great lover. I might sacrifice all of this, all that I have, for my love; sacrifice it without a second thought. My reasoning is flawless; my initial premise less so – which I can both recognise and deny, simultaneously. I am absent-minded. I don't notice obstacles in my path until the very last minute. I have become prone to flushes and hot sweats.

Alcohol helps the passage of the nights. What I would do without its assistance I have no idea. I would sit and think about her and go mad. I would go absolutely mad and thereby gain access to the unuttered truth of all our lives, the unreason that exists just below the surface of things. A privilege, perhaps; though on the whole I suppose I would prefer not to be mad.

I will walk past her desk again tomorrow.

I will look for her.

But if she is not there I don't know what I shall do.

Act 66:

1975, *Radical Philosophy*, an interview with Foucault, I was three years old. This isn't depressing, it's heartening and being able to mine whole caches of this stuff actually does something strange to time: The longer I download and speed assess, the less the time spent away from this stuff counts; I am reversing into that time, the time of my background coming out of nowheresville, a working class industrial family by the canal...

Act 67:

Stars judged as they die by people. Ananke the pitiless. Fuck right off. Wolf Son Professor. And the other one, the thin guy.

Rant 4

Something about death. In pop socks and tights with spots and polka dots pulled up high, higher than her later dabblings in the occult. Her racist friends. What memory does. The erasure. The early morning bed erasure of all of that stuff. The duvet; the sleeping-bag, the childhood blanket in dark green and red when you were warm, last. Lying there. The walk ahead. A void. Memory of. 80s pop synths and girl singers living on in the black slab, forever. All of history rendered instantly returnable by technology. The weight of that history.

Roy Bayfield even published a book under my name. If I had the money I would enter into litigation.

Act 68:

Gagarin died in a jet crash five years after that film, so modernism and its 'other side' are scripted in... There's a colour M62 film I saw but it's a bit out of Manchester really. The notes are written by Iain Baird who Sophie knows. Logie Baird, the black slab inventor's great grandson (I think). He didn't live on Buttershaw Estate, in 1974.

Act 69:

All of existentialism really has its roots in a romanticism that is trying to deal with the on-off of industrial life. The existential does not really have its roots in Heidegger but this, therefore the rural is the off to the intolerable unceasing on.

Act 70:

Transhumanism has its roots here too, so the first chip and first act of writing is meaningless, this is not an event when the on off machine was working way before then...

Act 71:

BMX days. 1984/5. Shade recreation ground, then visiting in the early 00s to find a tree growing in the quarter pipe we dug out of the hill. 15 years of age, we saw construction, they saw destruction, parents, council work gangs, chased us off, we dug the hole, the neighbours all complained about the hole, the council condemned the hole, got us banned us from our hole (!) But only nature filled the hole... twenty five years, then BLOSSOM!

Act 72: Mark-uh

Richard, it's the twenty fourth of January 2018 and Mark is dead.

Not interested in credentials – how many times anyone's seen them etc – yet not wanting to knock anyone's response plus, as well, wanting to shout my own credentials as loud as I can manage.

Maintain a silence.

Stunned, mainly, when the news comes through on Twitter. Later, my wife asleep, start to feel upset and cry.

Mark E. Smith's mind, spouting autopoetic babble across the airwaves, from the city which in turn spewed his lightning conductor figure. E. Smith, with foul-mouthed cronies, strange, slightly sinister cockatoos.

'The BOMB itself became content, having had a short reign as environment'.

- *Marshall McLuhan, Counterblast, 1969.*

The IRA device detonated in 1996 also survives as an urban myth mantra as 'the best thing that happened to the city'. In 24 Hour Party People, Tony Wilson unveiling the Hacienda club, likens the city to 'renaissance Florence'. Martin Hannett retorts with 'this is dark ages fucking Manchester'. The Wilson and Hannett characters present negative and positive images of the same place, a Janus head looking in two directions at once, a duality recurrent even before Friedrich Engels' pejorative study during an era of industrial pride. As Manchester's Annual Programme Group have pointed out, the city was viewed as an ill ripe for correction, a locus with no right to exist in its current incarnation, immoral, base. See Lowry – Corrie even – right up to novels like Acid Casuals.

Yet recent images of shiny bars and flats shore up this concrete oxymoron. The dualities are usually presented in tabloid binary form, 'Madchester', soon to be swallowed by 'Gunchester'.

E. Smith's glass is neither half full or empty, though it's often both. The Fall represent what the Manchester Area Psychogeography Group called 'the multi-real', in opposition to 'the Mighty Real'. Taking in every life form, '…homeless, addicted, or working and comfortable, all rub shoulder to shoulder in the flickering montage of meanings that is Oldham Street.' E. Smith stutters signifiers representing such polyphony, businessmen and bag ladies, 'young graphic designers!'. The monochrome LSD revelations of 'Jawbone And The Air Rifle' are horribly thrilling, lucid. He doesn't ever nail it, he tear-gasses it. 'Winter' is truly psychogeographic, a spatial exploration.

Feel a right idiot for crying. Don't know why I am. Suspect writing, even now, a couple of weeks later, about my tears somehow, in some way I'm not clear about yet am still, all the same, pretty certain about, undermines those tears, proves them false. Nevertheless…

On the night news of his death comes through I listen to the radio show which is playing Fall songs.

How would Mark E. Smith respond to this news is a question I keep asking myself, fully aware of the illogicality of the question. And I can come up with no firm answer. The days following there seems to be a mass of tributes appearing across old media and new. I'm pleased. It's nice to see. Surprised, a bit, at the same time though.

Mainly, during this time, I'm okay, every now and again though, on the tram, walking to work or something, I find the tears rising up and it hits me all over again. And immediately after such moments there is the embarrassment and the feeling like a knob. What can I do?

'M5' is weird, a whole angry day swallowed in two minutes through prismatic spectacles. Jeff Nuttall talked of how his 'ritual trance in the landscape was artwork of greater potency than the painting that was the proposed end of the exercise'. Smith lurks here, medicined, spouting Burroughsian paranoia like a tourette's shaman. A giggling, gummy imp on 'D.I.Y Meat'. He makes the song less important than the impression made, but his torn jotter places him closer to Cubism than Impressionism. Schwitters opening a Beefheart franchise in Blackburn.

Manchester is a malleable energy field. According to wave physics, three different results are possible: resonance, interference, or annihilation,

'I curse your family and wish them poor'.

- The Fall, Squid Lord, 1988.

I have attempted a couple of poems since his death

and each of them has proved shite. No different from the time before, my dad in Hope Hospital awaiting the operation for the cancer in his bowel, and I'm supposed to write something for that ridiculous Fall-themed poetry night in town, where I rush straight off to one night after visiting. My effort, hopeless. Rubbish.

Why can't I write about The Fall?

Do they mean too much to me?

Some other reason?

I don't know. I just know I can't do it. Though I'm forgetting that paper I wrote on Smith for that conference once…

The development of this current text went 'tragedy' first; 'pop-star death' second; 'Mark E. Smith's health' third, more mentions of and assorted buried references to The Fall fourth, before – finally – the real life news that this section of writing is responding to. I can't think about any of that right now though.

Walking to work, yesterday, with my wife, and we find ourselves talking about him again; plus talking about some kid my wife vaguely knows, an ex-boyfriend of her friend's daughter or something, some dude who topped himself; a topic which leads onto bringing Ian Curtis into the conversation. And for all the past misery of my life and talk of killing myself and attempts, even, at the same time I suddenly find myself with absolutely no patience for the idea of suicide. Getting angry at anyone who would do that to themselves. And again I'm back on Mark E. Smith, how he seemed to do just exactly what he wanted throughout his life regardless of what anyone might think, and the pair of us are crossing the old iron bridge over the Ship Canal, entering Salford from Trafford, and once more I find myself crying and getting annoyed at myself for doing so.

Later on, that evening, I learn, from Twitter again, obviously, that it had been Smith's funeral that afternoon. And there was a fight at the wake.

More myth: The proletariat pigeonholed as 'baggy', 'rave', only rose from its bed occasionally, to nick cool trainers to wear and/or sell for drugs. Then it cleaned up and shook hands with the Prime Minister. Northerners like Leeds' Gang of Four and events like the Red Wedge concert were the left wing hangovers of UK Punk and Rock Against Racism.

E. Smith's Manchester both conjures and contains the prowling back street monsters of that era. 'Behind the Counter', aggressive and wonky, a mid afternoon five pint binge, then back to the studio: The Fall continued to reflect a bleak, sardonic, dole queue north, even when the Oasis logo had replaced the Union Jack, rendered it obsolete.

The first time I saw The Fall: the difficulty I had convincing Moran to come with me. The difficulty we had deciding which night of the four-night residency we should attend. Us speculating as to the likely set-list. Both hoping – naively; very naively as I would come to learn – for Bingo Masters Breakout… Details I remember from that night are next to nothing. Just a general impression remaining of the scrum of the Roadhouse's audience, though whether that solely from that night or else some kind of composite memory from the other times I saw the group play in small, packed clubs I don't know… a packed room bouncing up and down to the songs. How addicted to that feeling I immediately became. Unlike Moran. Smith remained out there, a contingent nightmare that middle class children might stumble on in their search for thrills in a now-hip north. But as we have seen, The Fall are multiple. 'Lie Dream Of A Casino Soul' and 'Container Drivers' conjure both Lancashire hells and heavens. Ambulances and ambivalences. Through the many years until the last time I saw them: last year at Victoria warehouse; a short twenty minute walk from our new flat. Some one-day festival my wife hadn't been interested in attending until a few of her friends from work said they wanted to go and then she changed her mind; her friends subsequently going on to change their minds too and it just being the two of us. The pair of us almost deciding not to bother with the gig coz that's just the way things have gone with me the older I've got: live music has seemed to require more and more of an effort. We did go though and after all that waiting around the walk to the front of the stage to watch the group perform a tight, powerful set. Impressive as hell. Then the investigation, online, later, as to what that massive lump might have been on Smith's forehead.

'Chicago Now' promotes E. Smith's Calvinist work ethic where he appears to criticise it in 'Puritan'. Half full? Half empty? Sell-out? Neither, none, it reads like a perfect trajectory, a total body of work, no compromise of aesthetic in any period. 'Idiot Joy Showland' is ramshackle and note form, menacing.

Deleuzian smashed fragment as magnum opus. A lot of these versions are thus, the nature of the beast which spawned them, and so they appear definitive, itself another contradiction in terms.

- interlude –

6m ago Tory MP calls government Brexit advice to firms "extraordinary"

10m ago Maintaining customs union will sell UK's Brexit short, trade minister says

10m ago Putting pressure on May, Labour backs new customs union with EU

1h ago U.S. labour agency overturns major ruling, citing Trump appointee's conflict

1h ago Delta, United Airlines become latest companies to cut NRA ties

1h ago Georgia lawmaker threatens to kill Delta state tax breaks over NRA stance

1h ago Amid fresh Trump tension, negotiators seek progress on NAFTA

Act 73:

Everyone in the city, the neat garden, the window. Across the road at Westpoint the launderette, then the loop cyclist, runners, dog walkers, school children with or without parents at particular times. How many in the city?

Act 74:

And I raised my head and the sky was full of mandalas: various sizes; some rotating; some still. The sky alive with the circular motion of one-ness, inexpressible in words. The image-screen pulled back. My eyes burning with the glory of this glimpse of forever I'd been granted; this forever sky of rotating, humming motion which I stood beneath, all earth-bound worries and concerns forgotten along with all sense of who I was, where I'd come from and where I wanted to go. Whether I was one person or two or several persons or all persons in the world simultaneously and at once ceased to have any meaning for me whatsoever; at one with the mandalas of the heavens opening up above me, and then...

Act 75:

2017 was second hottest year on record, after sizzling 2016. 2018 was second hottest year on record, after sizzling 2017. 2019 was second hottest year on record, after sizzling 2018. 2020 was second hottest year on record, after sizzling 2019. 2021 was second hottest year on record, after sizzling 2020. 2022 was second hottest year on record, after sizzling 2021. 2023 was second hottest year on record, after sizzling 2022...

Act 76: Love and Happiness (more of the stuff)

The grey sky booms sodden with aeroplanes, the bus

trundles under them, sixth class transport, voices like windscreen wipers all around, but you are going to Her Place. Which means that some of these people are going to Her/His places.

'Opening their eyeballs eyeballs, pretending that they're Al Green Al Green.'

Act 77:

The lightning doesn't just flare where it strikes but briefly illuminates the rest of the territory. We don't just need Flash Fiction we need Flash Theory, Flash Theology, Flash Philosophy.

There is not enough time. We have enough at our disposal to do this. We are all in all of it: Fiction, Theory, Theology, Philosophy.

I sometimes wonder if I will go out in a Catherine Wheel of Flash Synopses, a Litany of things I wanted to complete but could not. But I have to make time to even make the Litany.

Like the moment when I knew I had two weeks left in the uni library and went down the aisles of books reading the blurb on the back of each one, I became exhausted with even that and had to sleep.

It will need a title for a start, something like 'Flash Synopses, a Litany of Things.'

A book on Provincialism. A book on Jeff Nuttall. A book on Marcuse (what's the point?)

Autoinfraography. An Autobiography through objects, cars I owned, clothes I wore, houses I lived in, jobs I had, institutions I attended. Clinically account for all of the infrastructural surroundings with the person removed and the personal will appear much clearer than if I had written a load of fuzzy 'memories'.

Text Generation Polemics. Generated Polemical essays using cliff edge books and random number generators. I did start this project very seriously.

Maybe Clocking Off and my Virilio essay for South Square can be one big book on time, along with my essay for J.D. Taylor's 'Theses of Digital Capitalism' and maybe my essay for the Castlefield show we did as Manchester Left Writers.

Lloyd George's survey on land ownership - a revelatory document about land ownership in Britain - about leasehold. Now that would be really good.

The Units What are the units? The Hour. One Million. The Couple. The trouble is it all drops out of the head and if you don't catch it it's gone and even the hastily scribbled notes add up to a book. Mortality.

Act 78:

In case you hadn't noticed, this work advocates the use of radical texts, intervening into the body politics of the neoliberal arts and humanities academy. The justification for this is that the so-called 'radical academic' and the supposed leftwing intellectual have so far failed to transform these problematic institutions and this is because their modus operandi has thus far been entirely positive, additive and 'molar' (Birrel, 1997: 109).

Its telos has been the stable mass of a body, not the molecular or atomic, let alone the disruptive atomic. Even critical negation serves no other purpose than to be filed in journals, in order to enable business as usual. Critical negation, then, here, is positive. It is also additive and molar.

Put more simply, art and academia - for those inside - is all 'ease' and no 'dis', if one takes the African-American slang for disrepect as the prefix of 'disease'. Here is a proposal to return the dis to the ease (y'all). There are theoretical forerunners to this argument which have not yet become reified, precisely because they are very hard to swallow.

Two of these are collected in Stewart Home's anthology of dissident literature Mind Invaders (1997). The first, Ross Birrel's Molecular (R)evolution explains that the '20th century has been plagued by 19th-century molar theories of evolution i.e Darwin and Marx.'

Birrel explains that 'Darwin's theory of evolution was molar as it was based on biological essentialism where the purity of structure was the basis of survival' (1997: 109). Marxist theory and philosophy 'was molar' Birrel adds, 'in that it assumed capitalism would naturally evolve into the pure state of communism', but 'these theories led to the Totalit-Aryan regimes of Hitler and Stalin' and now 'they have given birth to a new form of fascism known as the "New World Order"' (ibid). We move from the molar to the encancerated via Ross Birrell's later work, his manifesto 'Freedom Through Movement, Towards a Molecular Theatre', which ghosts the academic ancien regime's Deleuzianism. It contains the assumption that individual molecular flights can disrupt territorialism in a bad order. But this is all deterritorialization with no reterritorialization. It is all flight and no fight. It is the atom as ostentatiously free to do whatever it wishes.

This thesis has not 'gone too far', it has not gone far enough. I would add that Darwin and Marx could both be argued for as dialectical, but the legacies of their work are only further 'additive' philosophies aimed at molar health, of the 'functional' body politic, for capital.

Basically, it is all supposed to make a good workforce, including armies.

The second text to reconsider here, Metastasis by Matthew Fuller, argues against additive philosophy per se by making a case that cancer is revolutionary: Here is the runaway development of cells, that become more primitive as they divide. It is therefore the ultimate negation of post-industrial Western capitalist society. Fuller does not use cancer as a metaphor, he argues that cancer itself is revolutionary. 'Cancer is a betrayal from within' of the last site of freedom from capitalism, the body, just as it is finally breached. It may now be clearer why these dissident literatures are very hard to swallow. Here though, we wish only to use Fuller's challenging text metaphorically.

It is worth spending a little more time on these different philosophical figures and others like them. Molar and additive, after reading Matthew Fuller, can be said to have opposites in the distributed, heterogenous and subtractive. The social sciences and humanities have a per se additive sense to them. They also labour under the dominant assumption that their outputs must always become more nuanced, not less. They must never become more primitive.

The dominant and repeated metaphor of the surface that covers the whole is another philosophical figure to challenge: The 'layered' is a cosmetic thesis; pancake foundation dusted over with rouge and painted with lip gloss, the assumption is that the real authentic body lies under these surfaces.

This is not what Debord meant in *Society of the Spectacle*: It is not advertising, plus television and then 'the internet', as excited postgraduate first readings often testify; it is a total social state. The idea of the 'integrated spectacle' so far has been a layered metaphor. It has not been interruptive, deracinating, radiating or carcinogenic. It is not seen as molar either, but its consequences are.

The authentic body cannot be found under the spectacle, it is shot through by it and reproduced by it. The spectacle is tentacular, it is not a surface sheen. Everyday life is not merely hidden under a gloss, consumerism shoots through it like a nervous system. The consumer tentacularization of everyday life is a system of values. But the two are no longer interchangeable in any neat binary - spectacle, mediated by consumer capital; everyday life - are endlessly coiled together as Ouroboros, only Ouroboros as Octopii.

The social itself ends beyond the cosmeticization of politics and the neo-proles who are unready to attack the socially functionless status of contemporary art, even if most of them knew where to find it, or what it was. The thesis that mirrors this one - the positive to its negative - is the naive idea that under consumerism lies everyday life itself.

However, this simple rhetorical trope of the journalist, that of the mirror reflection, must also be ditched as itself a simplistic and lazy image from a past time. It is also the figure of the crude dialectic which must give way to aufheben in Hegel's fuller sense. But even this is not enough.

The tentacularization of everyday life manifests in claims from the historical neo-proles: That 'things are how they are because they are just how they are.' These claims must not be refused, as they are currently, by the liberal left. They must not be given the status of 'false consciousness' either, but allowed to burst into the Hegelian absolute. These claims must necessarily reach their 'full unfolding', not 'in' art, but in cosmeticism: Cosmetics into personality. Into the tentacularized arena of cosmeticism, not so much a 'manifestation' of cosmetic fragmentation, but a total phenomenon. This is the body politics of the neo-prole and nothing can intervene from within: Fuller advises the encanceration of the body, towards an autodestructive academia, the same monad stucture can be found in the neoliberal university: Molecules of knowledge move slowly from published paper to published paper, the whole body is stable, self-regulating, but, as Lacan said during a talk in 1967, the university is in fact geared precisely so that thought never has any wider ramifications outside the university.

Before navigating away, we must reflect and repeat that in any historical era there is no depth, only surface complexity. Metaphysics, of course, still gives the illusion of depth. 'Authenticity' and its status as doxa never interrupts its magnetic power for human discourse. It is worth also repeating that the social ends beyond the cosmeticization of politics.

Following on from Ross Birrell's manifesto, perhaps via Lyotard's Economie Libidinale, we must examine the body politics of homo academicus further: Its cells divide, but in a nutritive process which pulls in other material. The cells remain the same despite this. Cells can be classified in the following way: Science cells and humanities cells. These will not mix except in the case of the occasional science cell which will pull in a humanities cell. Experiments have shown that they can mix and produce healthy tissue, but this will not happen in the body unaided.

The autogenesis of new cells or even the hybridisation of old cells is a very rare occurence. Yet homo academicus testifies to this process almost constantly. This misunderstanding of her or his own body is one of the great mysteries of philosophy.

This brings us to conflicts within the psychic and physical organism. Psychic energy emerges from internal tension in the body. These tensions differ depending on the body in question. Psychic tension is produced when repressed physical tension is diverted. Anger, libidinal urges, the nutritive instincts and what we might describe under the shorthand of 'hunting'.

Emissions: Nutritive, libidinal and communicative. These come in three types: Solid, liquid and gas. Next, the whole assemblage raises itself from its chair to speak... and... and...

As Mr. C said in his pamphlet 'Towards the Last Gasp' (2016):

Such trash, chiff-chaff tales, littering every utterance: Public government, happiness and virtue in the Private Life, intentionally unprofitable pursuits. The Arts. These considerations, amounting to the settlement of the question for others, are not offered the phenomenon of sympathy here.'

Bataille would approve. Although this is not to say I am proposing the sun come closer to the earth in order to burn out our eyeballs so that we can no longer organise on the surface of the planet, even if by some sort of poetic serendipity this actually now appears to be happening.

Fuller's thesis m ps onto B t ille's when in concluding he suggests th t th t ll life h s degener ted from 'once glorious tumours' to our contempor ry c pit list version, in short, 'hum ns'. No, the problem is th t the work of homo c demicus h s thus f r been ' dditive' nd mol r. Let the bomb rdment begin.

W could think of th probl m through c nc r-c using r di tion. Mol cul s with n unst bl nucl us mit r di tion which c n nt r th body nd c us its c lls to r produc 'dysfunction lly'. If w t k this s m t phor for c d mic work, th probl m with it is th t thous nds of unp id hours of l bour go into m king it 'st bl ', into m king c

d mic work h v h rd nucl us, which do s not sh d lph

or b t p rticl s. Th h lf-lif is th tim it t k s for n obj

ct to d c y to h lf its v lu . Th n olib r l c d my is not

doing b d job t r ching this h lf-lif , but hop fully it

should b cl r th t I dvoc t t king up Birr l nd Full r

- t l st on m t phoric l l v l - so th t th n olib r l c d

my c n with r nd di .

F r t l ng c d m cs h v ss m d th t 'n g t n fr m w th

n' w ll s lv th pr bl m, f r t l ng th n v rs ty h s r m n

d m l r, s lf-s st n ng, s lf-r g l t ng nt ty. Th nc nc r t

n f th n l b r l b dy m st b ch v d by dm n st r ng d

sr pt v lph nd b t p rt cl s, s ch s th s n , lth gh th

p ss b l ty th t th n l b r l c d my s nt r ly c nc r-pr f

m st n t y t b d sm ss d.

X:

I say agane that I com to thea in a flaming of the spirit,

a vexation of the tongues only.

Moon an Sun... Beam of Wood... Coat... Bulock...

Onion... Cock an Hen... Key... Bookworm... Jackdaws

or Crows... Ice... Horn... Weathercock... Stormcock...

A One-eyed Garlic Seler...

At one zero hour...

...he provided for his friend

...he provided for his friend

...of his waist

...he provided for his friend

...he provided for his friend

...was thier thicknes

...he provided for his friend

...large

...not talents of ivory

...he provided for his friend

...he provided for his friend

...not minas of gold

x

Notes

Cut out the following and place them next to the passage where you need a note:

[1] [2] [3] [4] [5] [6] [7] [8] [9] [10] [11]

[12] [13] [14] [15] [16] [17] [18] [19] [20]

[21] [22] [23] [24] [25] [26] [27] [28] [29]

[30] [31] [32] [33] [34] [35] [36] [37] [38]

[39] [40] [41]

Here are the notes to the corresponding passage(s):

[1] Ibid.

[2] Preliminary considerations: There is an x which uniquely satisfies "f(x)" and that any such x satisfies "c(x)" where "f!(x)". Suppose someone, glancing in a certain direction, says (1) "The man walking into the pub is happy tonight."

[3] In fact Burroughs shot his wife, Althusser strangled his, or claimed he did.

[4] This is very different to some of the other things, that wanker who nicked the basic idea of a whole short story of yours and then got it published, that arsehole who took that thing of yours to a job interview and got the job partly by showing it. Some people are just straightforward cunts. You say *yes* because as Rotten once put it 'more fool them for only having one idea and that was somebody else's.'

[5] There are no bre

[6] Get thee to the gamblinghowce.

[7] The Fall, 1979.

[8] U don' kno du U? Du U U?

[9] Restored scene: if taking the train 2 hours 30 mins to go look at art always investigate thoroughly the website of the relevant gallery re the necessity, or otherwise, of booking ahead for the exhibition. "If this advice you choose not to follow there will be tears at the Barbican beside the long queue of wiser customers, the queue stretching all the way from the ticket desk to the Gents toilets three floors above you". Let no one witness your tears. Turned away from the exhibition of your choice, in abject and pitiful despair, you will be forced to 'try to make the best of things' by going looking at some other exhibition by some artists you have never heard of. Your misery will be compounded three-fold if you are accompanied by a friend from work. Misery experienced singly is never as bad as misery experienced doubled FACT.

[10] The Spinster: Enabler of this text's De Certeau reference, for the copy of *The Practice of Everyday Life* resting on one of the shelves of this flat, did indeed, once, a lifetime ago, belong to the famed spinster M. Ward, whom I met for the first time during a lengthy summit meeting held in the Cornerhouse bar after an initial correspondence carried out in the comments boxes of our respective Blogs (the title of mine now escaping me) occasioned by a piece I wrote on Patrick Keiller and skiving at work. Thereafter our paths continued to cross a number of times before rumours eventually reached me that she had abandoned the city for sunnier climes. It would, indeed, be a tremendous pleasure to be able to consult the spinster again.

[11] The Fall, 1989.

[12] Op cit. Cans of Barbican-ah.

[13] Hand rockin' good couple!

[14] Dig the hospital process.

[15] Holiday encounter middle touch list talk single...

[16] But Otherness does not mean some sort of trans-fantasy, it means Resistance. Premeditated, concrete resistance. Unreadiness to the point of total stoppage. This is the opposite of accelerationism. This is decelerationism.

[17] Negation of negation: - x- = +
[18] Since evil is here, haunting this world by necessary law, and it is the attitude's desire to escape from evil. We must escape. But what is this escape? It is attaining the entire nature grounded in virtue. But does not likeness of virtue imply Virtue to some? So we are returned to the concrete abstraction, real mirage, grounded illusion, and the great beast of a difficulty.

[19] But nothing is so simple after the Twentieth Century. It is now a long step forward from reaction to speech, at the same time as it happens much faster. From impulse to act, the signal to satellite leap occurs in a nanosecond, but in that nanosecond the signal passes through the noise and spacejunk of a hundred hyperaccelerated years.

[20] We cannot leap over this rubbish, we have to go through it. We do not have to face and go through a void, as Heidegger claimed, but wade into the accumulated rubble of the last decade. There is no 'around', no bypass road and no void either.

[21] The Fall, 2001.

[22] 'The object of this study is to examine the progressive

development of new social relationships through the constitution of "a phenomenology of occursus" which took place between some researchers during 2013.'

[23] These are not merely Exercises in Style.

[24] There are many contiguous lines and corresponding points in this book for The Reviewer. André Stitt, who he hung out with, Long Mynd, where caught short, he once had to strain at his stool plein air. Caerleon, where Arthur Machen lived.

[25] All those naughty Crusaders, re-appearing in legions on the *Daily Express* masthead. Sleeper Cells from the twelfth century staring at the same headlines about migrants and Strictly and Clarkson day after day after day.

[26] Put differently, one day we will all wake up, there are no Starlings left and everyone is an Individual and an American who speaks American English. You, me. Even the Chinese.

[27] Such trash, chiff-chaff tales, littering every utterance: Public government, happiness and virtue in the Private Life, intentionally unprofitable pursuits. The Arts. These considerations, amounting to the settlement of the question for others, are not offered the phenomenon of sympathy here.

[28] The Fall, 1985.

[29] 'Ross Birrell's manifesto *Freedom Through Movement, Towards a Molecular Theatre* ghosts the ancien regime's Deleuzianism. It contains the assumption that individual molecular flights can disrupt territorialism in a bad order. This is all deterritorialization with no reterritorialization. It is all flight and no fight. It is the atom as ostentatiously free to do whatever it wishes.

This thesis has not 'gone too far', it has merely not gone far enough.'

[30] Op cit.

[31] The Fall, 1988.

[32] Its seaplane violence assesses mortgages.

[33] Readability (Gunning-Fog Index): (6-easy 20-hard) 6.5

[34] 'Eskimo'.

[35] Behind Westminster X provided the memory wear, neither off Miss Y, which means it feels like the plastic of a blam of other drinking expel stop the through roads with sheets.

[35a] stolen time, stolen time! Reminiscence and nostalgia. SEHNSUCHT SEHNSUCHT SEHNSUCHT SUCKER!

[36] My own potential film, the illuminations of ash.

[37] Hallucinating apologia dismissal, deaths day pub frankness, or is the phone nuclear please?

[38] Up the gun, least chip these walked those old the growing Sunday aspects.

[39] Complexity Factor (Lexical Density): 44.8%

[40] Or (2) "the lady has made a profit".

[41] Sexual North towelling thaa having in it.

[41a] paraphrased and quoted from Foucault; one of the books of his left over from Sal's Msc.

[41] Skit: eventually, get where you're going. Downtown, New York. The 70s, 80s or maybe even the 60s, just the second half of the 60s. Dry your eyes son. This is a day away from work and you're looking at art and it's good. Get a cab home at half four in the morning; whatever you do, don't walk!

Index of First Lines

The Acts

Act 10: Date Night
'Withering academic claptrappers...' [...]

Act 11: Love and Happiness (reprise)
'I shit mesen...' [...]

Act 12: America
'Pregnant with promise and anticipation but murdered by the hand of the inevitable, belly split open like Rexroth wanted to...' [...]

Act 13: The newly present spiritual (England)
'Not some whiffy Sinclair-Ackroyd thing...'

Act 14:
'I do like a JPEG...' [...]

Act 15: Christmas
'The cunt next door...'

Act 16:
'Time for cheese...' [...]

Act 17: Melodrama
'Ditto...' [...]

Act 18: Twenty Eight Three Thousand Word Tragedies
'I had nothing to do with it... [...]

Act 19: More Tragedies
'My legs feel weak...' [...]

Act 20: towards a taxonomy of enjoyment
'Nor did I...' [...]

Act 21: Stockport post depot
'Fucking neckache literary pretention...' [...]

Act 22:
'A guy with a huge long Mercedes tries to park...' [...]

Act 23:
'The woman at the counter who judges with her face....'
[...]

*Act 24: The revolution will depend upon a flexible courier
service*
'Richard let's throw on dresses and wigs and get into town
in the name of the social sciences...' [...]

Act 25:
'The huge muck...' [...]

Act 26: Leaving Planet Ex
'But roots from momentarily...' [...]

Act 27: Returning to Planet Zed
'Manchester events made in didacticism have been
pissed...' [...]

Act 28: On preferring the American remake
'Coz it's funny' [...]

Act 29:
'My speaker liked your the violence, night night
inexpressible Nuttall.' [...]

Act 30: Unfilmed Michael Haneke script
'If to every in her glimmers through to the film of the
coming Christmas government...' [...]

Act 31:
'Richard form Hot Steven? Steven form Hot Richard?'
[...]

Act 32:
'Michelle Digital Trump 67 elongation any *Wire* ago' […]

Act 33:
'Soylent Green Weather' […]

Act 34:
'Joe grading the James girl up, he roams…' […]

Act 35:
'Our Circuit through…' […]

Act 37:
'Rigour, piano time ground…' […]

Act 38:
'A firm text photograph…' […]

Act 39:
'Steven form Cool Richard? Richard form Cool Steven?' […]

Act 40:
'Prolonged vehicle love…' […]

Act 41:
'Geraldine and the unlovely Attorney…' […]

Act 42:
'Is the overlooked time' […]

Act 43:
'The pure wank Churchill…' […]

Act 44:
'Downcast says the Dub…' […]

Act 45:
'However the kittens' temperature…' […]

Act 46:
'Nowheresville time now…' […]

Act 47:
'The coming remark of some gatherer…' […]

Act 48:
'The incomprehension partners…' […]

Act 49:
'The past biennial…' […]

Act 50:
'Massive badonkers' […]

Act 51:
'novels and slabs sold in Stockport' […]

Act 52:
'The totem importance of declaring ambitions you don't really have…' […]

Act 53:
'Pop star deaths rarely move me…' […]

Act 54:
'To those guy girl problems' […]

Act 55:
'Radical Philosophy' […]

Act 56:
'Ah cunt ghee a toss' […]

The Acts

Act 57:
'Old money, yes...' [...]

Act 58:
'Pretentious square brackets' [...]

Act 59:
'The alpha line narrative deserted and closing going-to-lunch town' [...]

Act 60:
'My shrieking chromatic background' [...]

Act 61:
'No ghosts here the sanitizer screened them...' [...]

Act 62:
'Tragedies paraphrase Russia death' [...]

Act 63:
'Korean i clones "don't cheap lies seem longer"' [...]

Act 64:
'Land mines for boy racers...' [...]

Act 65:
'The Act Circuit aimed at different dubs...' [...]

Act 66:
'Bullshit hatred piled overhaul mechanism...' [...]

Act 67:
'I say agane that I com to thea...' [...]

Act 68:
'And more brilliant object...' [...]

Act 69:
'How big is your custard-chucker, said…' […]

Act 70:
'Over-under…' […]

Act 71:
'No chance…' […]

Act 72:
'Knickerline aesthetics pomped up to baroque piffle by flash fiction writers of a certain age…' [Danny was right, he often is…]

Act 73:
'No Kreugerrands for David…' […]

Act 74:
'Richard, this is going to the publishers now: It is likely someone will return saying; "why don't you just give us The Acts and not all this other confusing stuff?" They will have missed the point, made when opening, with the use of Lacan, that one cannot act without others lurking, without the monstrous demands of the ego and id, without the botched attempts, backstories, misfires, rages, rants, sentiment, etc… And if you are writer this includes your mad methods, pitches, hedged pages, vomit. Therefore the Footnote to Act 74 is the last brown M&M in the bowl backstage at the Van Halen gig…' […]

Act 75:
'I say agane that I com to thea..' [...]

Act 76:
'Y TELL ME TELL ME WHAT TO DO…' […]

Dubs
Dub 1:
'Margarine complex fuddle...' [...]

Dub 2:
'Neo Elvis fling racket...' [...]

Dub 3:
'Chuck your muck said...'

Dub 4:
'The red drink separatist' [...]

Dub 5:
'No bitcoins for David' [...]

Exercises
- exercise 1 -
Watch two solid hours [...]

- exercise 2 –
Take two radios [...]

- exercise 3 – on undermining narrative coherence
'Hear ye this, ye' [...]

- exercise 2 –
'Timex is the gift...' [...]

Interludes
- interlude (meanwhile) –
58m ago [...]

- interlude (more on music) –
Bra straps [...]

- interlude (even meaner while) –
53m ago [...]

- interlude –
Spocky wocky [...]

- interlude –
52m ago [...]

- interlude –
58m ago [...]

Incunabula
- Work: LIVE BLOG (after Michel de Certeau) -
This is no pub quiz pedantry, p... [...]

- Vagina -
'Bayfield, the 'Fly by Roadie' [...]

- note to reader -
This [...]

Credits
Acts 3, 5, 8 and exercise 1 etc by Richard Barrett.
Acts 1, 2, 4, 6, 7 exercise 2 and interlude etc by Steve
Hanson. Act 18 by Richard Barrett and Steve Hanson.

I've lost track of the rest of it, and anyway all the
numbers have shifted as things were inserted. I even
began to actively enjoy it when Richard/Steve emailed
saying 'sorry I've buggered up the numbering again'. Plus
I've auto-changed so much of it I no longer know if I
wrote my own parts, or if someone else did. Stichard
Reve.

References

Adams, Tim (2018) 'London's Fatberg on Show: We Thought Of Pickling It' in the *Guardian*, https://www.theguardian.com/culture/2018/feb/04/fatberg-museum-london-display-pickling-age-waste [accessed 04-02-18]

Anonymous (1996) *Gilgamesh*. Harmondsworth: Penguin.

Ant, Adam (1982) *Goody Two Shoes*. 7". EMI.

Birrell, Ross (1997) 'Freedom Through Movement - Towards a Molecular Theatre' in *Mind Invaders* (ed Home, 1997) London: Serpent's Tail.

Birrell, Ross (2002) *The Theatre of Destruction: anarchism, nihilism & the avant-garde, 1909-1945*. PhD thesis. University of Edinburgh.

C, Mr. (2016) *Towards the Last Gasp*. Manchester: Pamphlet, no publisher listed.

Cormack, Cosgrave and Feltmate (2017) 'A funny thing happened on the way to sociology: Goffman, Mills, and Berger'. *The Sociological Review*, Vol. 65(2) pp. 386–400. London: Sage. No fucking idea either.

Elkin, Lauren (2016) *Flâneuse: Women Walk the City in Paris*. London: Penguin.

Fall, The (1990) *45 84 89, The B Sides*. London: Beggar's Banquet.

Fall, The (2005) *The Peel Sessions* x6 CD. London: BBC.

Fassbinder (1970) *The Niklashausen Journey*. Arrow Films.

Fassbinder (1976) *Satan's Brew*. Arrow Films.

Fuller, Matthew (1997) 'Metastasis' in *Mind Invaders* (ed Home, 1997) London: Serpent's Tail.

Hanson & Wilkinson (2012) *Steve and David Talk About The Fall*, Manchester: Nowt Press; https://nowtpress.files.wordpress.com/2012/07/the-fall1.pdf [accessed 03-02-18]

Fleischer, Richard (1973) *Soylent Green*. EMI DVD.

Foucault (1980) *Power/Knowledge*. London: Penguin.

Foucault (1988 [1961]) *Madness and Civilization*. London: Routledge.

Hanson, Steve (2017) A Book of the Broken Middle. Fold.

Hhassall, Llavery, Rraves (2012) *The Saga of Go-bert, Goberta and Gobertina*, Manchester: Nowt Press; https://nowtpress.files.wordpress.com/2012/09/nowt-071.pdf [accessed 03-02-18]

Kabakov, Ilya and Emilia (2017) *Not Everyone Will Be Taken Into The Future* http://www.tate.org.uk/whats-on/tate-modern/exhibition/ilya-and-emilia-kabakov [accessed 03-02-18]

Laing, R.D. (1970) *Knots*. Harmondsworth: Pelican.

Lavery, Carl (2013) *The Politics of Jean Genet's Late Theatre: Spaces of Revolution*. University of Manchester Press.

Leno, Dan (1902) *Spiritualism*. Windyridge.

Lyotard, J.F. (1974) *Economie Libidinale*. London: Continuum.

Manchester Confidential: *This is Manchester: 99 photos from the 1970s*: https://confidentials.com/manchester/this-is-manchester-99-photos-from-the-1970s [accessed 31-01-2018]

MAP (1995) *Multi Real vs. Mighty Real* at http://www.twentythree.plus.com/MAP/ [accessed 10-02-18]

McLuhan, Marshall (1969) *Counterblast*. London: Rapp & Whiting.

Michael, George (1984) *Careless Whisper*. Epic.

Musil, Robert (1996 [1942]) *The Man Without Qualities*. London: Vintage.

Nuttall, Jeff (1970) *Bomb Culture*. London: Paladin.

Nutt ll, J ff (1980) *P rform nc rt M moirs*. London: C ld r.

Pound, zr (1986) *Th C ntos of zr Pound*. N w York: N w Dir ctions

Pound, zr (1970) *Guid to Kulchur*. N w York: N w Dir ctions, Print.

---. Lit r ry ss ys of.

R t rs (2017) *Th W r* , D c 24. S m r p rt ng by B n Bl
nch rd n B j ng nd Hy nh Sh n n S l; dd t n l r p rt
ng by H j n Ch ; d t ng by Chr st ph r C sh ng, R b rt B
rs l.

S ss n, S sk   (1991) *Th Gl b l C ty*. Pr nc t n.

 pt n, L wr nc   (2012) *B n gn rt st c tr sp ss s m th d, nd
pr d ct n*, M nch st r: N wt Pr ss; https://n wtpr ss.f l s.w
rdpr ss.c m/2012/07/n wt-04.pdf [cc ss d 03-02-18]

Sp r ts

C pt n B fh rt & Th M g c B nd, b z r C pp , r c D lphy,
R b rt G l t , M ch l H n k , J ff K n , R l nd K rk, T l K pf
rb rg, G r ld n M nk, N g t vl nd, J ff N tt ll, Th R d Cr y l
, Th R d Kr y l , J hn R tt n, K n Sp rn , T ld Sw nt n.

T ls

 bl q Str t g s, T r t, Ch ng, Th R d Kr y l , J ff N n T xt
D b tw p nt wh t v r t s n w, nl n txt n l y s s, F n
d Ch ng f nct n n d b   n D s gn.

33985530R00162

Printed in Great Britain
by Amazon